Parker is in for a big surprise. . . .

"Hey, you guys," Parker murmured, holding out both hands. He was as mesmerized as he had been at Rolex by their strong, powerful builds and sweeping lines. Fanfaer, a bay with dapples, and Black Hawke, a black horse, were both by the same sire whose lineage went back to the legendary Welton line.

"What do you think of my newest purchases?" Brad asked, studying Parker's enraptured face with amusement.

Parker opened his mouth, then shut it. Then he opened it again. "But what are these two doing here? They're eventing horses, not racehorses," he stammered.

Collect all the books in the Thoroughbred series

Collect all the books in the Ashleigh series

*coming soon

THOROUGHBRED

PARKER'S PASSION

CREATED BY

JOANNA CAMPBELL

WRITTEN BY

KARLE DICKERSON

HarperEntertainment
An Imprint of HarperCollinsPublishers

HarperEntertainment
An Imprint of HarperCollins*Publishers*
10 East 53rd Street, New York, NY 10022-5299

This is a work of fiction. The characters, incidents, and dialogues are
products of the author's imagination and are not to be construed
as real. Any resemblance to actual events or persons,
living or dead, is entirely coincidental.

Produced by 17th Street Productions,
an Alloy Online, Inc., company

HarperCollins books are available at special quantity discounts for bulk
purchases for sales promotions, premiums, or fund-raising.
For information please call or write:
Special Markets Department, HarperCollins Publishers Inc.,
10 East 53rd Street, New York, NY 10022-5299.
Telephone: (212) 207-7528. Fax: (212) 207-7222.

ISBN 0-06-054441-4

First printing: October 2003

Printed in the United States of America

Visit HarperEntertainment on the World Wide Web at
www.harpercollins.com

❖ 10 9 8 7 6 5 4 3 2 1

To my mom, Gwyn

1

EIGHTEEN-YEAR-OLD PARKER TOWNSEND STOOD IN THE terminal at Kennedy International Airport in New York, a worn duffel bag slung over his shoulder, and studied the screen in front of him. "Flight four-oh-one to London, boarding at gate seven," he whispered out loud. A few hours earlier he'd watched his girlfriend, Christina Reese, ride her way to victory in the final leg of the Triple Crown on her horse, Wonder's Star.

Parker was thrilled that Star had won the Belmont, but he was doubly thrilled that he and Christina had decided to get back together. Their breakup certainly had been difficult, and he'd really missed her. Their becoming a couple again had made this whole trip worthwhile. Even though Christina would be spending the rest of her summer racing at Belmont and Saratoga, and Parker would be across the ocean preparing for Burghley, a prestigious four-star event held in England, they had parted with the agreement to keep their relationship strong. And he knew they would.

The previous night Parker had given Christina a tiny rhinestone horseshoe necklace that he'd bought at the track gift shop. "Here's something for good luck while I'm gone," Parker had said. "I'm sorry they're not real diamonds."

Christina had shaken her head. "I don't want diamonds," she said, her hazel eyes shining. "I just want you."

Just the thought that Christina was once again his girl had kept Parker smiling all the way to the airport. But now that he was about to check his luggage for the flight to London, something felt off. Not between himself and Christina—that was great. But something seemed . . . well, unfinished. He didn't feel quite ready to leave yet, but he couldn't figure out why. As he got closer and closer to the front of the line, he still couldn't figure out what it was, but the feeling was gnawing in the pit of his stomach. His eye drifted to a giant ad for Palm Pilots. The woman in the ad had bright red hair and a wide smile. "That's it," Parker whispered under his breath. The woman in the ad looked just like his mentor, Samantha Nelson. Suddenly a thought popped into his head, so quickly and so powerfully that he didn't have time to talk himself out of it. He knew what he needed to do.

"Next," the ticket agent called. Parker walked over to the counter with his mind made up. He quickly explained his new plan to the ticketing agent.

She handed Parker his revised itinerary. And Parker smiled.

He was going to go back to London, all right. But first he was stopping for a couple of days at home, in Kentucky. *I need to talk with Sam before I can go back. Forget England. I'm going to Whisperwood!*

He wondered if he was nuts, changing his plans at the very last second. *Maybe I am nuts, but I don't care. I need to see her*, Parker decided. He knew he couldn't leave the States without spending a little time with Sam and her husband, Tor Nelson. Together the Nelsons owned Whisperwood, a combined training facility near Lexington.

Jack Dalton will explode when he finds out, Parker thought, picturing his instructor back in England. He hoisted his duffel with its faded school crest onto the rack to be checked in for the flight to Kentucky. *But I have to go. After all, I'd never have been given the grant to train in England in the first place if it weren't for Sam.*

• • •

A day and a half later Parker stood on the edge of Whisperwood Farm's cross-country course, watching his favorite pupil, sixteen-year-old Kaitlin Boyce, take a couple of low fences.

"Hey, Brit boy! Check this out!" Kaitlin called as she pointed Sterling Dream toward an imposing jump that resembled a hayrack. She shielded her eyes against the hot June sun and glanced over to make sure that Parker was paying attention.

"Go on, I'm watching," Parker urged somewhat nervously. Kaitlin's warm-up gymnastics had gone smoothly, and when she had started jumping over a few practice jumps set up at the edge of the field, Parker hadn't given it a second thought. But now that she was about to take the dappled gray mare over the huge hayrack, drops of perspiration trickled from Parker's brow, sweat that had nothing to do with the Kentucky summer heat and humidity. The last time he had seen his former student approach a sizable jump like this, she'd sunk her weight into one stirrup, ducked to the right, and gone flying over the fence— without her horse! Luckily, she hadn't been hurt, but Parker definitely didn't want to see a repeat performance.

But this time Kaitlin and Sterling negotiated the difficult jump with ease and landed squarely on the other side. After she pulled up, Kaitlin pumped her fist in the air and whooped loudly. Parker clapped his hands together and emitted a low whistle. Twisting around in her saddle, Kaitlin grinned at Parker and took off her helmet in mock salute.

"Not bad, huh?" she joked as she brushed some wet tendrils away from her face. "I think I've finally broken my bad habit of putting too much weight in one stirrup."

Parker nodded. "It's a whole new you. Must be all that blond gunk you put in your hair," he cracked. "Makes all the difference."

Kaitlin shot him a look. "Ha ha, very funny. And I haven't used any blond gunk. My hair's just gotten sun-streaked since I've been out in the sun riding so much."

"Well, you two have *definitely* improved since I've been gone," Parker replied.

"Told ya we would. I'm dying to move up from prelim one day." Kaitlin patted Sterling's darkened neck, flecked with foam. "This sweet girl and I have big plans."

"Not so fast," Parker shot back. "You just rode prelim for the first time this spring, as I recall."

"Yeah, but I want to go into the advanced division, like you. I want to enter Rolex."

Parker grinned. "You will, one day. You can't rush these things. Just be patient and keep working."

5

"Yeah, right. Patient like you," Kaitlin said sarcastically. "Well, gotta go—time to get back to practicing." Kaitlin waved at Parker with her leather crop as she galloped off.

Glancing admiringly at the sleek, well-muscled Sterling, Parker smiled appreciatively. He loved England, but it sure was nice to be home.

Parker had spent the early part of that month in England, where he was training with British eventing instructor Jack Dalton on a United States Equestrian Team grant. Parker had been hard at work preparing for Burghley, a prestigious four-star event held in late August, when his grandfather, Clay Townsend, had surprised him with a plane ticket to the States. At first Parker had hesitated to accept his grandfather's generous offer. Parker and his horses had settled into a rigorous training regimen because he desperately wanted to be ready for Burghley. If he was ever going to get to ride for the Olympic eventing team, he had to make a good showing. But going back to the United States would mean that he'd be there to see one of the most exciting moments in Christina's life—racing Star in the Triple Crown. How could he pass that up?

When Jack Dalton had found out about Parker's plans to make the trip, he made no secret of the fact that he thoroughly disapproved. He didn't want Parker interrupting his training—especially not to sit on the sidelines watching a horse "gallivant around a track," as he put it. A renowned eventer himself, Jack Dalton had little interest in racehorses.

"Why fly over there when you can just watch it all on the telly and call your friend afterward? You told me Christina is your *ex*-girlfriend, after all," Jack had pointed out.

Parker had tried to explain that things were complicated between him and Christina, that though they weren't a couple any longer, she still held a very special place in his heart.

The instructor, who was known for his trademark British reserve, had raised his eyebrow at Parker's jumbled explanation and shaken his head in disappointment. Clearly, he just didn't understand.

"But Christina's dream of winning the Triple Crown is as important to her as my Olympic dream is to me," Parker had said. "I need to be there for her."

"Never mind all that," Dalton had said, waving his hand impatiently. "You need to be *here* schooling Foxy and Ozzie. Even though you just won that local horse trial on Ozzie, he's still dicey. He hasn't jumped consistently since then, and you've got to sort him out—or sell him to someone who can."

"Never," Parker had declared, swallowing hard as he thought of his problematic but talented mahogany bay gelding, Wizard of Oz.

7

Parker had bought Ozzie in April as a prospect, insurance in case Foxglove got injured. He knew that in order to be seen as a serious contender, a rider needed to bring along more than just one horse. It was very important that Parker sort out Ozzie so that he always had another mount in the wings.

"I won't need to sell Ozzie. He's going to work out. You'll see," Parker had told Dalton, faking a confidence he didn't feel.

Dalton had grumbled, "Well, he certainly won't work out if you don't put the proper time into him. And taking off for the States on a whim certainly isn't going to help matters."

"I'll train twice as hard when I get back," Parker had promised before dashing off to Heathrow Airport.

Once he was back in the United States, Parker had pushed his worries aside. He watched with admiration and pride as Christina battled her way through a difficult Triple Crown. First Star had gotten boxed in and had finished last in the Kentucky Derby. Then Star and Christina had gotten bumped in the Preakness. But in the end everything had fallen into place. Christina and Star had won the Belmont—the last jewel in the Triple Crown races. Parker was so glad he'd been there to watch Christina achieve her dream.

"And now I need to achieve mine," Parker said to himself as he walked away from the cross-country course and turned toward his mentor's office. "I've got to talk to Sam." Though he'd spent plenty of time in Sam's company since arriving at Whisperwood the day before, he'd found it very hard to pin Sam down for a real talk. And his need for a real talk was the main reason he'd decided to postpone his return to England in the first place.

Parker was determined to catch his former instructor and tell her what was really on his mind. First, of course, he needed to thank her for all the effort she'd put into working with him and his beloved mare, Foxglove, over the years. Being away in England and facing tougher international competition, Parker had come to appreciate just how much Sam had taught him.

And there was another reason Parker wanted to talk as well. He wanted to tap Sam's brain and see if she had any suggestions for unlocking Ozzie's potential. Samantha was known all around Lexington for her ability to handle difficult horses.

Difficult could certainly describe Ozzie. Though he sometimes showed the scope and talent over fences that had made him a winner of the Nations Cup before Parker had bought him, more often than not Ozzie showed his not-so-spectacular side. He refused fences for seemingly no reason. And sometimes he let himself out of his stall, galloping across the countryside and jumping everything in sight.

9

Just that morning Parker had called Dalton's stable to check in. Thomas, the groom, had mentioned that Ozzie had been larky the last few days. Parker knew that *larky* was the term the Irish groom used when Ozzie was really acting up.

Parker was concerned about Ozzie, but he knew he had to approach Sam carefully. He didn't want her to know just how worried he was. She had enough on her mind these days. After all, she was pregnant. And if she wasn't dashing out to give a clinic, she was schooling a young horse or frantically dealing with the latest crisis at Whisperwood. Parker didn't want Sam fretting about his horses and his problems on top of everything else.

It's still amazing to think that Sam is expecting a baby, Parker mused to himself when he saw his red-haired mentor staggering toward him, her arms full of supply catalogs and horse magazines. She looked slim and girlish in her jeans, as full of vibrant energy as ever.

"I've simply got to excavate my office. There are some papers in there from prehistoric times," she said with a smile as she caught sight of Parker. "But these dusty suckers are going to find a new home in the recycling bin. They've become more of a bug condo than anything. You should have seen the spiders that scurried out when I grabbed this stack."

10

"Let me help you," Parker said, leaping toward her and reaching to take the pile.

"Forget it, Sir Galahad. I've got these well in hand," Sam tossed back, a light laugh bubbling in her throat. She jerked her chin in the direction of her office. "But there are plenty more in there you can haul out if you want to help."

Parker saluted and headed toward Sam's office. As he ducked through the door, he caught a glance of his reflection in a small mirror covered with multicolored horse-show ribbons, noticing that his dark hair was damp with sweat and his smoky gray eyes were ringed with fatigue. Although he had tried to rest up over the last few days, he had found himself lying awake nights, worrying about Ozzie—and about whether he'd perform well at Burghley.

Everything depended on this big event. If he performed poorly there, the chef d'equipe for the United States Equestrian Team would probably withdraw the grant that enabled Parker to train with Dalton. Parker was certain of this much. But then where would that leave him? Sure, Parker could probably return to the University of Kentucky and finish up his studies, but that would probably be the end of his eventing dreams.

That was unthinkable. And his parents would certainly never let him hear the end of it. They had cut him off financially when he'd made it clear he intended to pursue eventing instead of taking up their offer to join them in the family business of raising and training racehorses. He could just picture his father's face when Brad gave him a well-warranted "I told you so."

Parker paused for a moment as he caught sight of a copy of *Bloodhorse* sitting on top of a chair piled high with magazines. His dad was pictured on the cover, standing next to his Preakness winner, Celtic Mist, under the Townsend Acres sign. The sunlight caught the sheen in his perfectly combed dark hair and the glint in his cold eyes. Parker's stomach knotted as he scanned the cover photo. It seemed that he could never escape his father's presence. Even now those eyes seemed to be taunting him.

You'll never make it as an eventer, Parker, the eyes seemed to say. *You were foolish to disobey me.*

Parker shook his head. *I'll be so glad to go back to England and get far away from him,* he thought. He had seen far too much of Brad lately, at Churchill Downs and more recently at Belmont. His father had surprised him by helping out his friend Melanie Graham when her horse, Perfect Image, had gotten injured in the Kentucky Derby, but Parker knew without a doubt that Brad had ulterior motives. Ever the opportunist,

Brad would never had offered to let Image rehabilitate at Townsend Acres' famed state-of-the art medical facility out of the goodness of his heart, that was for sure.

"No such thing as a free lunch, right, Pop?" Parker muttered, echoing one of his father's favorite sayings. He hoisted the stack of magazines up on his shoulder and stepped out of the barn office.

Turning to follow Sam, Parker caught up with her just past the barn entrance. Off in the distance he could see the cross-country course, where Kaitlin and Sterling were still practicing over fences. They were heading toward a particularly treacherous picnic table that required both speed and accuracy to negotiate. Parker paused for a moment, noting how boldly Kaitlin rode and how balanced Sterling appeared upon landing.

"Blaine's really helped Kaitlin improve," Parker remarked to Sam. He was surprised to hear the jealousy in his voice. It was his competitive side coming out. Blaine Delaney was the interim instructor who was filling in for Parker while he was away. But Parker didn't like anyone outdoing him in anything having to do with riding, even teaching.

"You just hate it when you're not the center of attention," one of his fellow eventing competitors, Lyssa Hynde, had once teased him. Parker hadn't taken offense; he knew it was true.

Sam shrugged. "Blaine's a great guy, but he doesn't have your touch. Kaitlin's improving because she's been working like a dog, trying to catch up with you."

Smiling with satisfaction, Parker walked along, his eyes traveling over the lush green pastures, where several gleaming jumpers munched on the bluegrass. Sam and Tor weren't rich, but still they'd managed to build a successful operation. Tor trained jumpers and steeplechasers, and Sam was in charge of the eventing side of the business.

At the sight of the empty pasture where Foxy used to be turned out for the day, Parker found himself wishing fiercely that his beautiful mare were there. He would have given anything to run his fingers through her cascading mane and feed her Polo mints, her favorite snack. Closing his eyes, he could picture her deep bay coat and her intelligent eyes. He could practically hear the distinctive shrill whicker that she usually saved just for him. He knew that Foxy and Dalton were getting along well, but that didn't stop him from missing her.

"Something's on your mind," Sam said, turning to Parker after they dropped their stacks in the recycling bin. "Let's go have some iced tea and talk. Cleaning my office can wait. It's waited this long."

Parker grinned. "Procrastination is a beautiful thing."

14

A few minutes later they were seated at the table in the Nelsons' cozy kitchen, Parker gulping a glass of iced tea. Sam took off her paddock boots, peeled off her socks, and wiggled her toes like a little girl.

"Well, spill it," she said after a moment. "Now that you've got that little British accent, I just love listening to you talk. So, how *are* things in merry old England?"

"Jolly good," Parker said, smiling. "In all seriousness, things really are quite good. I mean, you already know that Jack's amazing and that Foxy's going brilliantly."

Sam nodded and smiled warily. "But that's not the whole story, right?"

Parker bit his lip, wondering again if he should burden Sam with his troubles. "No, that's pretty much it," he lied.

Sam looked closer. "Parker Townsend, don't think for one minute you can fool me. I've known from the moment you turned up here the other day that something was gnawing at you. Out with it."

Parker sighed. "It's Ozzie," he blurted out. "I wonder if buying him was a huge mistake."

2

"WHAT DO YOU MEAN?" SAM EXCLAIMED. "OZZIE JUST won a horse trial against all kinds of really nice eventers that should have beaten him hands down. At the time I couldn't believe it. That was incredible."

Parker toyed with his glass. "That's just it. Ozzie's always incredible. But sometimes he's an incredible *pain*. Since then, he's been . . . well, *dicey*, as Dalton puts it. Just the other day he told me that Ozzie wouldn't even go into the stadium-jumping ring, let alone jump a matchstick. Later that same day he went through a jumping chute exercise like he was born to it."

Sam nodded. "That horse definitely has his ups and downs. One minute he's refusing all over the place, the next minute he wins his first horse trial—a jumper with no eventing experience, against all those seasoned horses. I can see why he throws you for a loop."

"You can say that again," Parker said. "And then there's the little matter of his escaping all the time, chewing up his blankets, and breaking his automatic waterers. He's a whole lotta horse, and even though we managed to do well at one horse trial, I have no guarantees he'll pan out the way I hoped he would." Pausing, he added, "Of course, I'd never admit that to Jack Dalton."

Sam shook her head and spoke gently. "But you knew that you were taking a risk when you bought Ozzie. You've only had him for a little while, after all. He simply needs more time to get to know you and trust you completely."

"The thing is, I don't have time," Parker exclaimed. "I've got to show my stuff now. I've got to show I've got more than one horse, or I'll never be selected for the U.S. Olympic team."

"That's not entirely true. Lots of riders are chosen who have just one horse," Sam pointed out. "But I'll admit, it improves your odds."

"I *have* to ride in the Olympics," Parker said, seized with passion.

"If it's not this time, maybe it'll be next time," Sam replied calmly.

"But you know the rumors, that the International Olympic Committee might drop eventing as an Olympic event," Parker shot back. "Maybe there won't *be* a next time."

"It's still just talk, and frankly, I can't see that happening," said Sam. "Besides, you can set your sights on all kinds of other prestigious international events. The Pan-American Games. The World Equestrian Games. There are lots out there."

"You're telling me to think long-term, right?" Parker asked thoughtfully, studying Sam's face.

Sam ran her finger around her glass and grinned. "You catch on quickly. I know this is hard for a gotta-do-it-now person like you," she said in a gentle voice. "But I truly believe Ozzie has what it takes. Remember, he's not going to become more consistent on your timetable. A great horse like him is going to do it on *his* schedule, and you just have to work with him steadily and have faith."

Parker snorted. "Easier said than done," he mumbled.

Sam fixed him with a look. "You of all people know that horses can't be muscled. They have to be finessed."

Parker bit his lip in frustration. Just as he was about to speak again, his cell phone rang. *Maybe it's Christina,* he thought. "Sorry—do you mind if I take this call?" he asked.

Sam shook her head, and Parker reached to answer his phone. He and Christina hadn't talked since he had left Belmont. Every time he tried her cell phone, he could tell that it had been turned off, because her voice mail picked up after only one ring. Parker knew Christina was busy, but he was aching to hear from her. Maybe she had finally been able to break away from her busy schedule to call him.

"Hello?" he said eagerly.

His heart thudded when he heard his father's imperious voice. "Parker, I heard you were in town. I need to speak with you."

Parker clutched his cell phone. How had his father known he was back in Kentucky and not in England? He had purposely avoided going to Townsend Acres so that he wouldn't have to subject himself to his parents' ploys. How had Brad tracked him down?

Don't be so naive, Parker, he thought. His father was powerful and had all kinds of ways to keep tabs on people when he wanted to. It was one of the things that had broken down their relationship in the past.

"Uh, now's not a—a good time, and, um, my cell phone battery is kind of low," Parker stammered, trying to keep his cool. It was never a good idea to betray anything that his father might take as a sign of weakness. That had gotten him into too much trouble over the years.

His father's cool laugh sent a shiver up Parker's spine. "Oh, I certainly didn't mean now, and I definitely didn't mean over the phone," Brad replied. "I'd like you to come over to Townsend Acres. Be here in thirty minutes."

Parker sat upright, his heart pounding in his ears. That was so like his father—to issue a command and not even consider that he might be busy.

"I'm sorry, sir, that's impossible," Parker stated automatically. "I'm in the middle of something."

"Whatever you're doing can wait," his father snapped. "This can't."

Parker stood up and turned his back to Sam, ashamed that she was witness to another of his family feuds. "I'm afraid that I am otherwise engaged," he said with exaggerated formality. "And anyway, I've got to be off to the airport in a little while."

"Nonsense!" thundered his father.

Parker was about to hang up on his father, but something made him hesitate. Did he detect a note of . . . desperation?

My father, desperate? How weird is that? Parker thought, struggling to figure out what to do.

Finally, without quite knowing why, Parker gave in. He sighed heavily, his shoulders slumping. "I'll be over," he said quietly.

Though he still had a few more minutes left in which to talk with Sam, he found he no longer was in any mood to think about Ozzie. He was too preoccupied with his dad's strange summons. Sam looked concerned.

"I wonder what dear old Dad wants this time," Parker mused.

Sam shrugged. "Maybe he just wants to show off the new stallion that he bought with Celtic Mist's winnings from the Preakness. I read about it the other day in the sports section of the newspaper."

"Maybe," Parker mumbled, though he was pretty sure there was more to Brad's call than that. Finishing his iced tea, he glanced at his watch, tempted to delay his departure even more. The idea of setting foot onto Townsend Acres made him want to hurl. "Go on, Parker," Sam finally said gently, rising from her chair. "Get it over with."

"Sorry to drag you away from your work for nothing, Sam," Parker muttered, standing up and taking his cup over to the sink.

"It wasn't for nothing," Sam said. "And I needed the break, even if I hate to admit it."

She patted Parker's shoulder in an understanding way and followed him out to his truck. Parker's mood blackened as he said good-bye to Sam and headed

21

toward Townsend Acres. *Dad wins another round,* Parker thought sourly, savagely slapping the steering wheel of his truck in frustration.

"Make my daaaaay."

Parker halfheartedly sang along with Melanie's boyfriend's band, Pegasus, on the radio as he turned into the gated driveway of Townsend Acres. But as his gaze rested on the huge brick manor house where he had once lived with his parents, his voice trailed off. It was no use trying to pump himself up. Belting out the upbeat tune that Jazz Taylor had written for his world-famous band just wasn't going to cut it.

Make my day? Parker thought with a snort, applying his brakes at the gatehouse his dad had recently set up as part of his beefed-up security plan. *More like* wreck *my day!*

"Name, please, and state your business," the uniformed guard barked out.

"Parker Townsend," Parker barked back in the same tone of voice. "Invited guest."

How else was he supposed to explain his presence? *Unwanted Olympic wanna-be? Semi-estranged son?*

"Who?" the guard asked, peering at him suspiciously.

"Parker *Townsend,*" Parker said, emphasizing his

last name. He didn't like to be rude to his dad's employees, but it annoyed him that the staff turned over so quickly that no one ever seemed to recognize him. He couldn't blame people for leaving, considering the way his parents treated them. But it still was annoying to have to introduce himself every time he came to his own family's farm.

The guard entered his name into the computer on his desk and waited till the word *cleared* popped up on the screen. Handing Parker an ID badge, the guard admonished him to wear it while he was on the premises. "Security first," the man said crisply.

"I promise I won't steal Dad's precious Preakness winner," Parker said sarcastically as he made his way onto the grounds of the stunning facility. Fighting the urge to turn around and head to the airport, Parker instead gazed at the impeccably bred horses dotting the vast fields around him. Mares from all over the world were shipped here to be bred to Townsend Acres' famous stallions. Now they and their foals were gamboling in the fields, creating a scene straight from the glossy brochures his dad distributed wherever he went.

No doubt about it, Townsend Acres was spectacular with its rolling hills and vast expanses of perfectly manicured bluegrass. Sleek horses grazed in the many roomy paddocks on the premises. As far as the eye could see, there were freshly painted white fences bordering fields filled with shady, leafy trees.

Parker slowed his truck and studied the newest addition to the farm, the medical facility. It was a gleaming testament to the latest in veterinary technology. Just recently Melanie and Jazz's horse, Perfect Image, had been treated there after her Derby injury. Now Perfect Image was rehabilitating, and Melanie was staying in the yellow guest cottage on the grounds.

Hey, maybe I'll bump into Melanie and Image, Parker thought, brightening. It would be nice to see a friendly face while he was there.

Parker's attention shifted toward the building that housed the therapeutic pool just as a stable hand led a black horse through the wide door. Parker squinted to see if it was Image, but from this distance he couldn't be sure. The horse looked like a tiny black speck. It could be any of several black horses in training at Townsend Acres.

Driving on, Parker could see activity in the training oval—the same oval where over the last few years he had seen a number of Triple Crown and stakes winners get their start. This day Parker saw that several large tour buses were parked in the stable area. Ever since Celtic Mist had won the Preakness, the tourists had begun swarming like horseflies to Townsend

24

Acres. His father's farm was now a permanent fixture on Kentucky's legendary horse farms tour.

While Parker parked his truck behind the huge buses, his eye traveled to the large barns that were designed to match the colonial style of the manor house. He had to admit that the place was beautiful, especially now that it was summer and flowers were blooming everywhere. But it was all about show and image. Parker couldn't help wondering if the tourists felt the same feeling creep into their bones that he did when they looked closer at the glittering horse facility. Beautiful but cold—that was how almost everyone Parker knew described Townsend Acres.

But Parker knew that Townsend Acres hadn't always been such a sterile, soulless place. At one time his beloved grandfather Clay had run the farm. Back then the place bustled with activity, just as it did now, and it commanded the same respect. But in the old days Townsend Acres had had beauty *and* soul. The horses had seemed happier, and the workers had also seemed to have more enthusiasm for their jobs.

One of his father's employees approached him now. He was a sour-looking man with thin, tightly pressed lips and a superior attitude. He was wearing the Townsend Acres uniform: a polo shirt with the farm's crest on it, a name tag, and crisp, creased khakis. Even though he was addressing his boss's son, the worker made no attempt to be friendly, and his eyes slid over Parker without expression. He looked down at Parker's ancient paddock boots, which were held together with duct tape, and sniffed disapprovingly.

"I left my good boots in England," Parker said defensively, and the instant the words came out of his mouth he regretted them. Why should he care what anyone, especially one of his father's snobby employees, thought of him?

"Ah, so that explains it," the man said. Then he glanced at Parker's face. "Mr. Townsend is busy being interviewed for SportTV right now, and he'll be occupied for quite some time."

Parker couldn't tell if the guy expected him to be impressed. Parker shrugged. Inside, however, he began to stew. How like his father to demand he arrive at a certain time, and then keep him waiting just to flex his power!

I'm not going to play his games, Parker thought savagely. "I'm outta here," he told his father's employee. "Tell your boss buh-bye. I've got a plane to catch."

The employee's expression changed rapidly, showing real alarm. "But you can't go. Mr. Townsend says to wait."

"No can do. Gotta fly," Parker quipped.

The man dropped his voice. "Uh, I probably

shouldn't tell you this," he said, "but the guard at the gate has instructions not to let you leave unless Mr. Townsend okays it."

Parker felt his head throb. He was being held hostage—by his own dad! *Well, what else is new?* he thought, his shoulders slumping. "Fine," he said between gritted teeth. "I'll wait."

3

"MR. TOWNSEND REQUESTS THAT YOU WAIT FOR HIM IN THE library," the worker added. Turning on his heel, he strode away.

In spite of his bad mood, Parker couldn't help being a little bit amused by the man's snobby attitude. It was the trademark of almost every person who worked at his parents' farm—and those who weren't snobby were excessively polite to him, fearful of losing their jobs.

Except for Connie. She was one of the maids, and she had a soft spot for Parker. She always went out of her way to be cheery and helpful.

That's it, he thought. *I'll go see how Connie's doing. There's no way I'm going to wait in my father's stuffy old library. If he wants to see me, he can come looking for me.*

Parker made his way to the large southern mansion, glancing at the cavernous garage past the graveled motor court and noting with satisfaction that his mother's late-model Mercedes was nowhere to be seen.

Good, he thought. *Mother's probably off at some garden party, acting out her usual role as the lady of the land and bragging her head off about the Preakness win. I don't need to bump into her, that's for sure.*

Parker had never quite gotten used to having a haughty socialite for a mother and a cruel tyrant for a father, but there it was. Lavinia and Brad were his parents, and just as he had his problems with them, it was clear they had their share of problems with him, too. As far as they were concerned, Parker was way too headstrong and stubborn. All through his childhood Parker had chafed at their tight rein, hoping that he could get his parents' attention. He wanted desperately for them to treat him lovingly and cheer him on as he pursued his dreams—even if what he wanted didn't mesh with their dreams. But Brad and Lavinia were determined to run his life while ignoring him at the same time.

As Parker had grown older, he'd realized that he needed to get out from his parents' iron grip, and so he'd moved in with Sam and Tor at Whisperwood. But after doing so, he'd felt conflicted and had even moved back home to try to smooth things over in the name of family peace. But now that he was eighteen, he had no illusions. He knew that he and his parents would never be close, though sometimes he couldn't help wishing it were otherwise.

Why am I even here? Parker thought as he let himself into the manor house. He winced as his dirty boots echoed on the highly polished marble floor in the entryway. Parker headed automatically for the kitchen. As he approached, he detected the comforting smell of blueberry muffins. And that meant Connie wouldn't be far away. Sure enough, a few seconds later she emerged from the connecting butler's pantry. Her face broke into a smile as soon as she saw him.

"Parker!" Connie cried with delight as she dashed over to envelop Parker in a welcoming hug. "You're just in time for some home cooking."

"I knew I smelled something delicious coming from this part of the house," Parker replied happily.

Connie pushed a few muffins off the cooling rack onto a plate and handed it to Parker, frowning a little. "From the looks of it, you could use a few more muffins. What's the matter? They not feeding you properly in England?"

Parker forced a laugh, determined that Connie not see how upset he was. "Are you kidding? Every time I turn around, someone's heaping food onto my plate.

30

Dalton's put me on a strict eating regimen. All healthy stuff. Protein and fiber—and lots of it. Guess I'm getting thinner because I've been riding a lot—and running to build endurance. Training two horses is more than twice the work of one, you know."

Connie patted his shoulder in a motherly way. "Well, you keep right at it. You go at it hard enough and you'll get what you want. I'll be watching you on TV in the Olympics one day. I feel it in my bones."

"I hope you're right," Parker said earnestly. *More than anyone can imagine*, he added silently.

"In the meantime, eat a few of these and get some padding on those bones!" Connie exclaimed.

Dalton would kill me if he could see me eating this, Parker thought, lavishly spreading butter on his muffin.

"So tell me all about things in England," Connie said. "You like the weather and everything over there?"

"Well, it *does* rain a lot, even in summer, but overall it's going well," Parker replied as he ate. "I've made some good friends. I really like working with Jack Dalton, and even though Ozzie can be quite a puzzle at times, I had a pretty nice win on him at a local horse trial held at this really cool English country house called Merebrook."

Connie beamed. "That's great!" she exclaimed.

Parker described the event in great detail, knowing

that Connie never tired of hearing about his riding endeavors. But though he talked lightly, all he could think of was how worried he was about Ozzie and how angry he was that his father had summoned him.

"And tell me about those people you're staying with," Connie said when he'd finished telling her all about his wonderful horse.

"The Chillinghams are the best, even if they are 'descended from one of England's oldest families,'" Parker declared in a fake English accent, imitating the way his mother said it when she wanted to impress her friends. "But they have this granddaughter that I could do without. Her name's Fiona." Wrinkling his nose, he told Connie about how the fifteen-year-old had been careless with Foxy at Merebrook and how as a result Foxy had gone temporarily lame.

"The worst thing is that now Fiona has decided she's horse crazy. She follows me everywhere like an annoying little sister," Parker complained.

"You could use a little sister," Connie replied firmly. "Being an only child has to be lonely sometimes."

Parker grinned and shook his head. "How could I be lonely with all the little brothers and sisters I've managed to acquire at Whisperwood?" he quipped.

Connie swatted at him playfully with her dish

towel. "Lesson students don't count. They *have* to do what you tell them."

Parker snorted. "Not true. They hardly ever listen to me," he said. He was thinking of how he said the same things over and over to some of his students, and still they didn't seem to hear him.

"I don't mean that exactly," Connie retorted. "What I mean is that it wouldn't hurt you to learn to share attention. Parker Townsend, you've always got a place in my heart, but you've got to admit you take up all the air in a room sometimes. You need a sister to humble you a little."

There it was again, Parker thought. Someone else telling him he was an attention hog. Still, he knew that Connie was only being motherly, so he didn't feel insulted.

"You can be sure Princess Chillingham isn't about to share any attention with me," Parker replied. "She's amazingly spoiled, and her grandparents dote on her. She's dying to prove to her grandfather that she can take care of his horse, The Lion, so she pesters me all the time to teach her about horses. At the same time, she does everything in her power to turn the stables upside down!"

Connie grinned, then shook her finger at him. "You be nice to that girl. She has feelings, too, even if she's got the princess thing going. And maybe she can learn something about horses from you."

Parker swallowed his last bite of muffin. "Oh, I'm nice to her," he assured Connie. "I even agreed to let her turn out Ozzie and Foxy on their days off while I'm gone. But secretly I made a deal with Phillipa Woodhall—she's one of Dalton's stable hands. Phillipa agreed to watch over her to make sure she doesn't do anything boneheaded."

Connie nodded approvingly. "Then it's all the way it should be."

"Fiona has written me letters every day since I've been gone," Parker added. "Good thing my cell phone doesn't take international calls, or she'd be calling me all the time."

"Sounds like someone's got a crush on you!" Connie exclaimed, her eyes twinkling.

"You think so? Well, she's definitely not my type, and besides, I'm taken," Parker said, chuckling. "Christina and I got back together!"

"That's wonderful," Connie said. She was clearly pleased. "I've always thought that Christina is a very nice girl, and she helps you see things straight."

While Connie washed up after her baking, Parker helped dry, and he and Connie talked about the comings and goings at Townsend Acres. From what she said, nothing much had really changed since he had left, other than the increased security measures.

"Of course, now that Mist won a Triple Crown race, there are so many more tourists," Connie added, looking out the window as a tour bus rumbled past.

"That ought to make my folks happy, I guess," Parker replied.

Parker thought he heard Connie say, "Nothing makes your folks happy." But right about then she dropped several baking trays, and amid the clatter Parker wasn't sure he had heard right.

"There you are, Parker," came his father's disapproving voice from behind him. "My, my, playing kitchen maid with the hired help. Really, I think Ms.—uh—I think she can handle it herself. That's what we *pay* her to do."

Parker froze as his stomach tightened. Spending time with Connie had calmed him down a little bit, but just hearing his father's voice made him anxious all over again. Parker composed his face before he turned around, so that it didn't reveal how much he hated the way his father had just put down Connie by forgetting her name.

"Hello, sir," he said coolly. Instantly he wished he hadn't automatically added the *sir*.

"I specifically ordered that stable hand—what's his

name—to tell you to meet me in the library," Brad said, looking at Parker in annoyance.

Parker nodded and flashed back to the stable hand's name tag. "His name is Jeff Gaines. And he *did* pass along your message."

"Which you thought you'd ignore?" his dad said, raising an eyebrow.

Parker nodded defiantly. "Um, yeah, that pretty well sums it up. I was hungry."

Parker saw Brad's eyes flicker for an instant. Then his face relaxed as he smiled widely, revealing even, white teeth.

What's he up to? Parker thought automatically when he saw the smile that reminded him of a shark's grin. *I hope he didn't order me to come over here for the sole purpose of ragging on me again about eventing.*

"Well, it's good to see you, son," his father said. "Come. Let's go take a long, leisurely stroll around the old horse farm, shall we?"

"Why?" Parker asked bluntly.

Brad pretended to look hurt. "Anything wrong with the old man wanting to take a walk with his son?" He turned on his southern accent thicker than ever.

Parker turned to follow his father out of the kitchen, hating himself as he did so. It irritated him no end to follow any order of his father's. Walking through the kitchen door, he turned and mouthed to Connie, "Bye. Thanks." She gave him a look of sympathy and waved him on with her dish towel.

Parker had long, lean legs, but he had to scramble a bit to keep up with his father's huge strides. Brad said nothing as they approached the stable area. Brad watched the stable hands scurrying about raking the immaculate aisles, and Parker noted how his father's eyes swept critically over to the training barns. Parker knew that no detail escaped his father's notice.

They walked past the stallion barn just as the most recently hired stallion manager strode by leading a monster-sized chestnut horse. Pulling against the lead, the horse stopped to paw at the ground, his huge hooves churning up the rich dirt. He let out a trumpeting neigh that seemed to rattle the windows.

"Some horse, huh?" Brad said. He reached out to touch the stallion's immense shoulder. Though the stallion had a stud chain on his halter, he lashed out violently at Brad with ears flattened and a malevolent look in his eye.

Leaping out of the way, Brad chuckled and waved the stallion manager on. "That ball of fire is my newest acquisition," he said proudly. "King's Ransom. Stakes winner. Bit of a dirty temper, but he's got good bloodlines."

"Another one of your bargain-basement finds?" Parker joked weakly, turning to look at the stallion's stunning conformation.

"If you call a few million dollars bargain-basement," Brad replied. "But I got lucky. The racing business has been particularly good to me this year. The owners needed the money, so I got him cheaper than you might think. And he's going to make me a bundle. Already got his book filled for the season."

Parker had stopped listening. He just wasn't interested in racehorse breeding. Instead his mind was back in England, where he was imagining himself tearing across a cross-country course on Foxy. He could practically feel himself astride her powerful frame, hurtling along. He could hear her breath coming in rhythmic puffs as he centered her toward a towering fence—a wide footbridge with a serious ditch underneath, or maybe a solid ascending ramp, just to keep things interesting. Brave and bold, Foxy was game to jump anything. He could feel the wind whipping his face and practically taste the tears streaming from his eyes.

Parker heard the sound of a swift kick and a metal bucket clattering onto cement. Someone shouted, "Knock that off!"

His mental picture dissolved instantly, and Parker was annoyed to have his pleasant daydream interrupted. *You'll be with Foxy very soon*, Parker told himself as he returned to the unpleasant reality of Townsend Acres.

Parker caught up with his dad and fell into step beside him. Parker could tell that Brad's attention was elsewhere. After a few minutes he and his dad took a turn that brought them by the training barn. Brad pulled out a small spiral notebook and quickly jotted something down.

Someone's going to get their pay docked, Parker thought, wondering just what was amiss. That was Brad's customary punishment for workers who made a mistake. *Ha, maybe this time it'll be Ralph Dunkirk.*

Ralph was the head trainer, and Parker had never liked him. When Christina's horse, Star, had been at Townsend Acres for training, Ralph had been really rough on Star. Though Parker hated to see anyone punished or fired, he couldn't help secretly wishing that Ralph would finally get the ax. Ralph, however, always seemed to beat the odds and had been at Townsend Acres for years.

Probably because his nasty methods dovetail so nicely with Dad's, Parker couldn't help thinking. Both men were harsh and inclined to do whatever it took to get quick results.

Brad put his little notebook back in his pocket without a word.

Though Parker was in a hurry to leave for the airport, the silence was making him even more uncomfortable. He groped for something to talk about. "So, how was your TV interview?" Parker asked, his voice sounding forced.

Brad pushed back his dark hair, the sweltering sun playing off his aristocratic features. "It went well, of course—once the reporter let me handle things," he said arrogantly.

Parker nodded, not sure how to reply to such a self-serving statement.

"I hear tourist traffic's picking up now that Celtic Mist has won a Triple Crown race," he said, making a further attempt at conversation while he darted a nervous glance at his watch.

"Mmm, and they want to see the Derby winner, too, even if she is broken down," mumbled Brad, referring to Image. Parker hoped his father would fill him in on Image's progress, but he didn't. Instead, Brad walked on, his eye twitching nervously.

Parker noted the twitch. *Jeez, Dad sure is acting weird about something.*

Whatever it was, Parker just wished his dad would spit it out so that he could get to the airport and fly back to England. Looking around Townsend Acres brought him no pleasure at all. Racehorses, as far as the eye could see. They were nice enough, sure, but just not his style.

I miss Foxy and Ozzie, Parker thought despairingly. His gaze drifted to a far-off field where a couple of Thoroughbreds were grazing under a stand of trees. From this distance, the two dark horses looked like dots. Parker drew nearer, and then his breath caught in his throat.

Naw, he thought, squinting in the sun. *Couldn't be. Could it?*

But Parker's eyes were telling him the truth. There in front of him were Black Hawke and Fanfaer, the two incredible eventing prospects he'd seen while at Rolex in April. At the time they had been for sale, but Parker had done nothing more than admire them from afar. It had taken only one glance at their impeccable conformation for Parker to know that they were well beyond anything he could ever have afforded.

Still, though Parker had had plenty to think about during the days he was at Rolex, he hadn't been able to help feeling a surge of excitement whenever he stumbled across the horses around Kentucky Horse Park. Every time he went to the concession stands or to check the leader boards, it seemed everyone around him was buzzing about these horses and their incredible lineage.

"English-bred," Parker had heard someone say. That had made his ears prick. After all, Foxy was English-bred, too.

One afternoon Parker had paused to watch a couple of potential buyers take the two horses over a few fences in one of the practice rings. His heart had practically stopped when he saw what beautiful movers they were and, though green, how fearlessly and easily they had jumped.

"Would you look at that bascule?" one British rider had uttered reverently. "It's an international crime. They never should have let horses like these leave the United Kingdom."

"They sure can jump, but you haven't seen anything till you've seen them in the dressage arena," an Australian rider had replied.

Sure enough, when Parker saw Black Hawke and Fanfaer being tried out in the dressage arena, they were power and grace. One day they'd be racking up impressive scores, without a doubt.

The last he had heard, his friend and fellow competitor David Breen had had his eye on them. But even David, rich as he was, had gulped at the asking price.

As Parker and his father approached the paddock fence, the horses lifted their well-shaped heads, and Parker caught a glimpse of their large, intelligent, liquid eyes. Both horses' coats gleamed in the sun, and they ambled over to the fence on long, muscled legs.

"Hey, you guys," Parker murmured, holding out both hands. He was mesmerized by their strong, powerful builds and sweeping lines. Fanfaer, a bay with dapples, and Black Hawke, a black horse, were both from the same sire whose lineage went back to the legendary Welton line.

"What do you think of my newest purchases?" Brad asked, studying Parker's enraptured face with amusement.

Parker opened his mouth, then shut it, like a fish gulping air. Then he opened it again. "But what are these two doing here? They're eventing horses, not racehorses."

4

"THEY MOST CERTAINLY ARE *NOT* RACEHORSES," BRAD sniffed, not even trying to mask his disdain. He paused and then said in an offhand tone, "They're yours. I bought them for you. Happy belated birthday. Merry Christmas. Happy Easter. Do you like them?"

"What?" Parker felt the blood drain from his face. His father had never bought him a horse in his life! It had been his grandfather who had bought the English-bred Foxy for him, and his parents had been furious when they found out. They would have preferred that Parker crawl to them, begging for the things he wanted. That way they'd have had control over him.

But even after that, Brad hadn't let up. While he knew he couldn't stop Parker from taking up eventing, he'd done his best to complicate things. First there was Brad's plot to send Parker away to study business. But Parker had stood firm and refused to go. Then Brad had tried to belittle Parker, putting down eventing every chance he got. But in spite of this, Parker had risen in the competitive sport until he had succeeded in winning a coveted USET grant. When Parker had announced his intention to go to England to train, Brad cut him off without a cent. But even that didn't deter Parker. He was determined to do things by himself. Still, there were definitely times when Parker could have used some extra money for his horses. Yet Parker would have sooner given up entirely than ask his parents for money—not that there would have been any point. Brad had made it quite clear that as long as Parker pursued eventing, he was on his own.

So why the sudden change of heart? Parker wondered. But the question flickered away as he looked at the two magnificent horses in front of him.

Hawke heard something rustle in the nearby trees. He stood like a statue, head up, nostrils flared. His body shuddered as he let out a shrill, trumpeting neigh.

He looks like something out of a storybook, Parker mused.

Fanfaer's ears swiveled toward the sound, but being the calmer of the two, he merely stood alert, eyes searching the trees for an imagined enemy.

45

"I just got them, so they're still getting settled in here. Their lineage goes back to the legendary Welton line," Brad bragged unnecessarily, since Parker was already well aware of the horses' lineage. "For sport horses, they're bred to the purple, that's for sure."

Parker nodded, unable to hide his excitement. "Everyone in the business knows about the Weltons. They've made real names for themselves in all levels of international three-day eventing," he said almost prayerfully. "Did you know dozens of them are internationally ranked. One of them, Welton Romance, is the only mare ever to have won a major eventing championship." He stopped himself, aware that he was letting on to his dad how impressed he was.

Brad shrugged. "Nice, if you go for that sort of thing. And now they're yours."

But Parker could tell that Brad couldn't help but being proud that he owned horses of this caliber, even if they were eventing horses. Turning to the exquisite horses in front of him, Parker found himself memorizing every detail of their magnificent frames. For a few seconds all he could think about was the fact that by simply nodding, these amazing horses could be his.

Get a grip, Townsend, he told himself sternly. *Remember, there's no such thing as a free lunch—especially not when it comes to dear old Dad.*

Parker turned to square off with his father, straightening himself up to his full height.

"Why did you buy them for me? What is it you want me to do?" he asked.

Brad looked blank, then made a show of looking hurt.

"That's a heckuva way to say thanks for a present like this," he said, evading Parker's question. "Look at Black Hawke's knees, will you? They're good as a racehorse's knees—big, flat. Perfect."

"What's the catch, Dad?" Parker persisted.

"No catch, son," Brad said, smiling.

It was a smile that Parker had seen too often before, one that was all in the mouth. His eyes remained as cold as ever.

Parker turned away and let his gaze rest on the two horses again, trying to keep his heart from racing. *Man, they are beautiful,* he thought longingly. Wouldn't Jack Dalton be impressed if he returned to England with these two? Wouldn't the Olympic committee have to take notice if he could bring horses like these to the team?

But Parker knew better than to lose himself in a hopeless dream. It could never be. There was no way he could accept them from his father. Turning, he faced Brad again. "Well, thank you, but no thank you," he said, struggling not to stammer. "I can't accept these."

"All right, then." Brad's jaw twitched, but otherwise he didn't change his expression. "But the least you can do is ride them before you go."

Parker glanced at his watch. "I would love to," he said. "But I have a plane to catch. I'm heading back to England, you know."

"Planes are almost always late these days. You have time," Brad replied. With that he raised his hand imperiously, and as if by magic, a stable hand appeared with tack Parker hadn't seen before at Townsend Acres—an eventing saddle and a bridle.

"Come on, you know you want to," Brad pressed almost teasingly, motioning the stable hand to hurry.

Gritting his teeth, Parker tried to stand firm. He knew that by riding Hawke and Fanfaer, he was bound to fall even further in love with them—and he simply couldn't afford to. But as he looked again at the horses, everything else was pushed from his mind. His eyes lingered on Hawke's strong hindquarters, rippling with muscle, and his flowing ebony tail cascading out behind him. The big horse stood just over seventeen hands, and his friendly horsy face seemed to beckon Parker.

"It can't hurt just to jump on for a few minutes," Parker mumbled. Taking the saddle and bridle from the stable hand, Parker turned to the horses. Admiring

Fanfaer's beautifully sloping shoulder, he made his decision. "I'll ride Fanfaer first." The stable hand darted between the rails and took hold of Fanfaer's gleaming leather halter. Leading him over to Parker, he swiftly helped Parker tack him up. While Parker buckled the well-oiled girth, he took note of Fanfaer's generous barrel and well-sprung ribs. Up close, he couldn't overlook the horse's long, strong legs with their broad, flat cannons and square, straight knees. Foxy was gorgeous and Ozzie powerful, but this horse was commanding in his own way.

Parker cupped his palm and took a few seconds to allow the horse to softly bump his hand. Running his hands over the big bay, Parker stroked him under the chin and gently massaged his sloping shoulder. It was important, Parker knew, to let the horse get acquainted with him before swinging onto his back. And sure enough, within a few seconds Parker got the sign he had been waiting for. The big horse let his ears flop and brought his head down, equine body language for acceptance.

With that, Parker led the horse over to a large rock and stepped up. He placed his boot into one stirrup and brought his other leg smoothly over Fanfaer's back. Settling easily into the saddle, Parker picked up the reins. Instantly he felt the horse's body quiver with anticipation.

He wants to rip, Parker thought with delight, recognizing right away that this was a horse that loved his work. Eagerly he turned Fanfaer toward the center of the paddock, away from his father's probing eyes. He didn't want anything to spoil the moment. Riding a horse such as this was sure to be pure joy.

When he had ridden a distance away and had found a flat area, Parker opened his fingers on the reins, directing the big horse to track left and move forward at the walk for a few minutes. Fanfaer's walk was swingy yet comfortable. Changing rein, Parker gently asked for even more impulsion at the walk and felt the horse come up underneath him. When the horse was warmed up, Parker cued him to trot, gradually engaging him even more from behind. Parker executed several walk-trot transitions and then worked at bending Fanfaer around his leg. At each request the horse responded willingly.

Finally Parker asked the big horse for a working canter. As he felt the horse's smooth, three-beat gait under him, Parker grinned broadly.

Absolutely amazing, Parker thought. Soon he was lost in the age-old dance of horse and rider communicating perfectly. Parker remembered hearing some old horsemen call it "having a conversation."

I've just got to jump this big guy, Parker thought, turning the horse toward a fallen log. It wasn't very high, maybe three foot six, but it rested on a slight bank, with a drop behind. It would give Parker a clue as to how the horse might handle a trickier jump.

Fanfaer's ears pricked, and he took hold of the bit as Parker tried to center him on his approach.

"Five, six, seven," Parker counted, automatically employing his crest release just as the horse tucked his legs up and soared into the air.

The jump was so scopey, Parker was almost left behind.

Parker patted the horse's neck after he landed. "Well done, boy," he murmured, feeling a rush of emotion as the horse negotiated the drop without missing a step.

He took a few more jumps and then reluctantly turned back toward his father and the stable hand, who held an impatient Black Hawke. The big black horse was pulling against his lead and seemed eager to get out onto the field himself.

Within minutes Parker was mounted on Hawke and headed back to the same flat area where he had just put Fanfaer through his paces. Hawke was a different ride. He was more nervous and high-strung, but he too loved his work and seemed eager to please. When Parker had worked him sufficiently over the flat, he aimed Hawke toward the fallen log.

Not a great approach, Parker thought as the horse

51

collected himself uncertainly for the takeoff. *But it was my fault. He needs more support on the left rein.*

Turning to take the fence again, Parker closed the left rein slightly, and Hawke balanced himself perfectly. This time he took the jump with ease.

"Good boy!" Parker exclaimed, drawing him up after he had landed on the other side.

Jump after jump, the game horse exhibited his desire to please. Parker felt a surge of exhilaration that he had felt only a few times before. He resisted the urge to whoop and instead quietly rode the horse over to his father. Being on these horses had been sheer heaven.

The things I could do on these horses! he thought ecstatically.

Parker's brain kicked into fast-forward. Here was insurance in case Foxy, heaven forbid, ever got hurt. Here was backup in case Ozzie didn't work out. These horses were green and might take years to bring along, but they had the potential to be real international eventing horses one day—beauty, breeding, and brawn all wrapped up in two neat equine packages.

Four horses? He suddenly caught himself. How could he ever manage to bring along four horses? It was all he could do to handle Foxy and Ozzie. Their training and fitness regimens took every waking minute.

But maybe that wouldn't be a problem. Parker's mind raced on. He could bring them to England and have Jack Dalton work them and get them fit while he continued working with Ozzie and preparing Foxy for Burghley. The minute Burghley was over, he could take over their training. Four horses would be an amazing amount of work, that was for sure, but Parker felt certain he could do it.

I'm thinking long-term, just like Sam suggested, Parker mused, patting Hawke's sweaty neck. Some of the best international eventers had all kinds of horses to ride, he reminded himself. But they also had grooms and assistants to help. That meant money—money he didn't have.

I'm the son of one of the richest men in Kentucky, and I'm flat broke, he thought ruefully.

Well, he would just have to earn it somehow. He'd get sponsors, the way Lyssa Hynde had.

Smiling, Parker pictured himself traveling all over the world with his horses. He would compete in all the best events—Badminton, the World Equestrian Games, the European championships. He could practically hear the roar of an appreciative crowd as he delivered a clear on some far-off cross-country course, riding for his country. He could almost feel the heavy medals clanking against his chest.

He'd stand on a dais and wave to the crowds.

Afterward he'd walk over to his proud parents and thank them for making this all possible.

But suddenly Parker glimpsed Brad from a few yards away and thudded back to earth. From this distance Brad looked as though he were chiseled out of granite. His face was stern and unyielding. A kind of savage power seemed to emanate from him as he sized up Parker.

You're mine now, Brad seemed to be saying.

What am I thinking? I must be out of my mind! Parker thought in a flash. *I know exactly what kind of man my dad is. I've known it for years.*

"Don't *even* think about these guys, Townsend," Parker said under his breath. "There's a price to pay—one that you can't begin to afford."

5

PARKER STARED STONILY AHEAD AS HE DROVE AWAY FROM Townsend Acres. He was still shaking from the scene that had occurred after he had told his dad that he would definitely have to turn down the gift horses. Apparently Brad had thought Parker wouldn't be able to resist after riding them. But Brad had been wrong. It had pained Parker to do so, but he'd refused them.

Brad had quickly dismissed the stable hand in a gesture Parker knew so well.

Never discuss anything in front of the help. That was one of his parents' mottoes.

Brad had raised his voice the minute the stable hand had led the horses away and was out of earshot.

Parker had stood his ground even though Brad had unloaded with astonishing force.

Standing quietly under the verbal onslaught, Parker nonetheless felt himself bristling with rage. Yet he spoke calmly, repeating his refusal while thanking his father politely.

"Why am I not surprised? You're being absolutely ridiculous, as usual," Brad had said as his parting shot before stalking away.

Parker had walked slowly to his truck, engulfed in misery. Perhaps he *was* being ridiculous. After all, his dad had said that he expected nothing in return.

If only I could believe that, Parker mused.

Driving toward the airport, Parker tried to turn his mind toward Foxy and Ozzie, back in England. These two horses were his, no strings attached. Wasn't that enough for him? So what if they weren't all-out glorious? They still were pretty great. Foxy had power, strength, and beauty, and over the years she and Parker had formed an unbeatable bond. And Ozzie, while he had his quirks, was loaded with potential.

Parker decided he was better off focusing on what he had than ruminating about what he didn't have. And he was just beginning to feel a little better when suddenly he noticed a state highway patrol car in front of him beginning to zigzag across all the lanes of the highway.

The officer is creating a traffic break, Parker realized. *There must be something on the road up ahead.*

Parker glanced nervously at his watch as he came to a stop along with the other cars on the road.

"How did it get to be so late?" Parker muttered. If only he hadn't stuck around to ride! Drumming his fingers against the steering wheel, he watched the minutes tick away while traffic still remained blocked.

"I'm going to miss my plane!" Parker said aloud to nobody.

Parker started biting his lip. He *couldn't* miss his plane. He just couldn't! Dalton hadn't understood in the first place why Parker had interrupted his training to go home for the Triple Crown. He'd been even more disapproving when he heard that Parker had delayed his return in order to stop off in Kentucky. If Parker missed his plane, Dalton would be downright furious.

Just as Parker thought he would explode, the officer signaled for traffic to resume, and Parker shot forward, but he only got about fifteen feet before he had to press down on the brakes. "Come on, come on," Parker cried, the tension building.

Traffic inched along all the way to the airport. When he finally got there, he parked quickly and sprinted through the terminal. "Oh, no! Another one!" Parker said out loud when he saw the long line of people in front of the security checkpoint. Getting through security took forever, and Parker got to his gate just as the British Airways jet taxied down the runway.

No, it's not possible, Parker thought in numb disbelief. He stood helplessly watching the plane take off. *Dalton is going to chew my head off!*

Perhaps he could get on the next flight? Darting over to the ticket counter, Parker explained the situation to the agent. The trouble was, the next few flights to London were booked solid.

"I'm afraid the best I can do is put you on an afternoon flight that leaves on the seventeenth," the ticket agent said.

"The seventeenth?" Parker cried. "That's two days from now! I can't wait that long."

The agent, an older, balding man, simply shook his head. "I'm sure you realize that in recent times there's been a real cutback in the number of international flights. It makes it harder when you have a last-minute change of plans like this."

Parker swallowed. It hadn't been a last-minute change of plans. It had been a rotten set of circumstances. But that realization didn't change anything. His plans to return to England had been dealt another setback.

"Don't blame anyone but yourself, Parker Townsend," Parker muttered to himself. He knew he should have been on guard. He never should have allowed himself to be taken in just because of a couple of beautiful horses.

"You're sure I can't do anything else?" Parker hounded the agent. "Standby, even?"

The agent shook his head. "I wouldn't advise standby. There are plenty of people already ahead of you."

Reluctantly Parker changed his tickets to the flight on the seventeenth. He frowned as he paid the penalty fee. *Money that I don't have,* he thought despondently. *Money I'd have in a heartbeat if I'd just give in to my dad.*

"Forget that!" he muttered aloud, resisting the urge to kick a nearby trash can.

A while later Parker was on the road again, heading back the way he had come. *Well, one thing's for sure,* he thought. *I'm not going back to Townsend Acres.*

Picking up his cell phone, he punched in Sam's number. "Can you stand having me bunk at your place again for a couple of days?" he asked after explaining to Sam what had happened.

"Of course we can stand it!" Sam exclaimed. "We're always happy to have you, Parker. Don't get all lathered up about your delay. Your horses are being taken care of, and anyway there's just nothing else to do about it. Look on the bright side—we can finish our conversation."

At least there's that, Parker thought grimly after they said their good-byes.

59

When he arrived back at Whisperwood, Parker headed toward the barn office. Sam was on the phone with the vet but nodded when Parker wrote a note asking her if he could use the other phone at the house to call Dalton to explain the delay.

Not that I'm looking forward to making this call, he thought, turning toward the house.

Parker picked up the phone in the Nelsons' cozy kitchen and dialed the number. It was early morning in England.

"Morning. Jack here." Jack's voice was crisp and clear.

Does the man never sleep? Parker wondered.

"Jack, it's Parker." Parker took a breath and went on before Jack could get a word in. "Look, I'm still in the United States. I missed my plane, and I won't be able to get another one until the seventeenth." Parker decided not to explain what had happened. There didn't seem to be any point in going into details. Anyway, Parker knew his instructor had no patience for excuses of any kind.

"Well, this is a bit of a bother, isn't it," Dalton said, sounding annoyed.

Parker knew the mild words didn't match up to what Dalton was really thinking—that Parker Townsend was undoubtedly the biggest Yank flake he had ever met.

"It couldn't be helped," Parker exclaimed defensively. He twisted the cord and wished that he could end this conversation quickly. Even from thousands of miles away, the instructor's disapproval came through loud and clear.

"I'll just have to keep sorting out your horses till you get here, then," Dalton said heavily. "But it's not the same. They need *you*."

Parker winced. "I'll take over the minute I get back," he promised, overwhelmed with guilt. He hated the idea that he was making more work for Dalton and the people who worked at his stable. They were all desperately overworked as it was. What was worse, Foxy probably missed him like crazy, and Ozzie might even be missing him, too. "I'll work twice as hard to make up for the lost time," Parker added, lamely repeating his earlier promise.

Dalton hung up with what sounded like a harrumph, and Parker's heart sank as he replaced the phone in the cradle.

Parker stood up and sighed. Now what was he to do? He had two days with nothing planned, no schedule to keep, and no horses to ride. It wasn't like him to be idle. He'd just have to find a way to keep himself occupied. Though it was late in the day, there was still plenty of light left, and Parker knew that things around Whisperwood were still amazingly busy.

Walking outside, he saw Tor shoot past with an armload of unpainted planks.

Probably fixing fences, Parker thought. *I could offer to help him, but he'd probably shoo me away.* Parker knew that Tor preferred to work on his own.

I'll go watch Blaine give a lesson, he thought.

Walking to the arena, he saw Blaine in the center mounted on Bentley, giving a late-afternoon lesson to several young riders over some stadium fences. The ever-helpful Kaitlin was scurrying around the arena and replacing the poles as they were knocked down.

Trying to kill time, Parker watched the lesson for several minutes before he headed toward the barn. The barn was hopping, as usual. Several kids were rolling bandages in the barn aisles, two or three students were cleaning tack, and even the barn cat was purposefully stalking a mouse that was scurrying toward the feed room.

Everyone sure is busy around here, Parker thought. *I'm the only one who seems to have nothing worthwhile going on.*

In addition to the jumpers and eventing horses Sam and Tor had in training, there were several sales prospects and a large number of lesson horses on the property. The staff more than had their hands full giving all these horses the attention they deserved. *Might as well make myself useful,* Parker thought as he saw the young riders returning from the ring. He watched students untack and begin grooming their mounts and felt a pang of jealousy. Wandering over by Sterling's stall, he watched Kaitlin crooning into the gray's ear as she fluffed up the mare's bedding and wrapped her legs for the evening. It was obvious how much she loved her horse.

I should be in England taking care of my horses, Parker thought as he kicked at a pebble on the ground. Sighing, he watched the pebble clatter down a drain.

Blaine came riding up on Bentley, a Clydesdale-Thoroughbred cross that belonged to one of Tor's clients, and Parker walked over to meet him.

"Looks like I'm back for a couple of days after all," Parker said. "Need any help around here?"

"Do I ever," Blaine said, grinning and dismounting. "I've been teaching nonstop all day, and I've still got one class to go before it gets too dark. Do you think you could make sure this motley crew puts their horses away properly and then school Scooter?"

Parker grinned back. Scooter was a smart lesson horse that was famous around Whisperwood for testing his riders whenever he was jumped. Generally only the strongest junior riders rode him, but even so, the personality-laden cocoa-colored gelding could outwit them by cutting out at a fence, throwing in an ill-timed buck upon landing, or hauling off around the course. When Parker had still been giving lessons, he'd had to climb on Scooter every so often and remind him of his manners.

"You bet," Parker said. He suddenly felt very eager to ride a familiar horse, even one usually used just for lessons. Blaine led Bentley down the aisle, and Parker followed him toward Scooter's stall, sidestepping several chattering students.

As Parker turned the corner by the crossties, holding Scooter's lead, he collided with one of the new girls, a ten-year-old named Lisette. She had started riding at Whisperwood just after Parker had left for England.

"No running," Parker said automatically, holding the lead tightly as Scooter spooked sideways.

Lisette's eyes widened, slowing only a little. "But Penny's chasing me with a bucket of yucky tack-cleaning water!" she wailed.

Just then Penny burst into view, running down the aisle, brandishing a bucket that was decorated in wild colors and painted with Chili's name.

"You just wait, Lisette," she shrieked, her face red and her pigtails flying as she ran toward the other girl.

Parker held his free arm across the aisle, blocking her. "Knock off the horseplay, Penny. You know the

64

barn is no place for that kind of kid stuff," he barked, trying to look serious. "You guys already spooked Scooter. Do you want someone to get hurt?"

Penny's face flushed with anger as Lisette ducked into a nearby empty stall. "But Lisette called me a bad name," she yelled, holding up the bucket threateningly.

"It wasn't a bad name!" called Lisette from the doorway of the stall. She stomped her muddy field boot for emphasis and got ready to slam the door if Penny should come closer.

"Was too!" Penny shot back.

Parker rolled his eyes. He wished Connie could see him now. She'd have to agree that dealing with his riding students was sometimes exactly like dealing with bratty little sisters.

"Calm down and let's discuss this," Parker said to the two girls. He waved away several other students who had crept away from their horses in the crossties and were watching the quarrel, their brushes dangling in their hands. "Get back to your horses," he called firmly to them.

Looking back at Penny, he asked, "What name did she call you?"

"I can't say it!" Penny exclaimed, pouting.

Parker sighed. "Out with it," he said, wishing he were on his way to England, or anywhere but there playing baby-sitter. "What did Lisette call you?"

"A—a hippophile!" Penny spat out. "And I'm going to give her a soaking she won't ever forget!"

"A *hippophile*? That's what she called you?" Parker bit the inside of his cheek to keep from laughing. Tweaking one of her pigtails, he whispered, "I've got news for you, Pen. Lisette didn't call you a bad name. She called you a horse lover, a horse enthusiast. That's what *hippophile* means."

Penny looked at him doubtfully. "Are you sure?"

"Very sure," Parker said. "You can look it up in a dictionary if you don't believe me. Now toss the water in that bucket down the drain in the wash racks and go take care of Chili. He had quite a workout today, from what I saw."

Penny's attention shifted. "Did you see me take him over the brick wall?" she asked eagerly.

"Yes, I did." Parker laughed. "Impressive. Now scoot."

Penny moved off reluctantly, and soon Lisette emerged from the aisle, sauntering down the aisle and laughing hysterically.

"Could you believe how mad Penny got over nothing?" she hooted to the other riders.

Parker sighed as he hitched Scooter to the crossties and got to work grooming the cocoa-colored gelding. While he worked the soft body brush against Scooter's summer coat, he let his mind drift. Soon he was mentally replaying his thrilling ride on Ozzie over the cross-country course at Merebrook. Surprising everyone, especially Parker, Ozzie had negotiated the challenging course as though he had jumped cross-country all his life. What a day that had been! Parker still cherished the rosette he'd won. It symbolized Parker's belief in the talented but inconsistent horse.

"He reminds me a little bit of you," Parker said to Scooter as he picked out the gelding's feet and tacked him up. "More talent than most, but with a few bugs to work out."

Scooter snorted softly as Parker mounted and rode toward the arena, which was now beginning to fill up with Blaine's next lesson students. Giving the students the rail, Parker started off on the inside in a businesslike manner, getting to work right away. He knew that students sometimes tended to start Scooter off at a lazy walk, which immediately gave the wily horse the message that he could catch his rider off guard. Nudging the horse's sides gently but firmly with his heels, Parker asked for a long walk. He changed rein, tracking right, after a while so he could work both shoulders.

When it was time to ask for a trot, Parker brought Scooter under him and asked for impulsion from behind. At the canter, he could feel that Scooter had gotten in the habit of speeding up and slowing down on whim. Parker knew it was important to maintain a consistent pace and ask for the variations only when needed.

When it was time to jump, Parker took Scooter out of the arena and headed for the cross-country course where earlier he'd watched Kaitlin school Sterling. Scooter's ears pricked up as they drew closer to the fence. It was clear the horse wanted to jump.

Just like Black Hawke and Fanfaer, Parker found himself thinking. Shaking off his thoughts, Parker tried to concentrate on Scooter, taking him over fence after fence.

Afterward he patted Scooter's damp neck and walked him around the large field as the evening shadows began to steal over the landscape. Scooter was no Foxy or Ozzie, that was for sure, but he was a willing animal, and once Parker got his attention, the horse tried his best.

As he rode back to the barn, Parker pictured Foxy and Ozzie, his heart sinking with every step. How was he going to get through the next two days in Kentucky knowing that he belonged in England with his beloved horses? Was he going to blow his chance to ride for the Olympic team?

Suddenly a thought crossed his mind. It was so startling that he pulled up momentarily on the reins, bringing Scooter to a full stop. His dad had tried his best to stand in the way of Parker's dream once again. It was just like when he'd tried to send him to school in Italy so that he wouldn't be able to event. It was merely a different way to complicate Parker's plans. There was no doubt in Parker's mind that Brad's ploy with the two horses had been a deliberate attempt to sidetrack him from getting back to England and continuing with his training.

Dad won another round. Parker knew his father was used to winning at whatever he set out to do. He could just picture Brad reveling in his latest success.

Well, he won the battle, but he's not going to win the war! Parker thought darkly.

6

THAT EVENING AFTER DINNER PARKER WENT TO HIS ROOM over the garage and called Christina on her cell phone.

Answer, please answer, he thought, frowning while it rang and rang. He realized he hadn't spoken to her since he left New York and that she didn't even know he'd gone to Kentucky instead of returning to London.

"Greetings from the beautiful Bluegrass State," he joked weakly when Christina answered. Just hearing her voice made him feel a little bit better.

"You're not in England?" Christina sounded surprised.

"No, I'm at Whisperwood," Parker said. "Long story—bad luck and a change of plans."

70

"Maybe it's not such bad luck after all. I had a change of plans myself. I'm in the Bluegrass State, too—back at Whitebrook," Christina said. "I felt funny, staying on to ride other people's horses in New York when my own horse was at home without me after running the race of his life. I decided I needed to fly home and make sure Star is settled in again before I go back to Belmont. But what happened to you?"

Parker toyed with the strap on his duffel bag. "My dad, that's what happened."

"Oh, no, not again," Christina exclaimed. She had known Parker's family all her life, and she had seen firsthand what Brad could be like. For one thing, Brad had meddled with Star from the time he was born.

"Yes, again," Parker replied.

"Tell me what happened," Christina said, stifling a yawn. "Sorry, I'm kind of wiped out," she added. "The airport was a mess, and I just landed. I'd come over to see you, but Ian's short of exercise riders, and I've got to get up early and help him breeze a set or two."

"Don't worry about it. I'll come over to Whitebrook tomorrow and tell you the whole sorry story," Parker said. He knew Christina had to be tired. She had been incredibly busy getting Star ready for the Triple Crown, and immediately afterward she'd begun racing horses for other trainers. It was an intensely demanding schedule, guaranteed to leave anyone

71

beyond exhausted. Parker didn't want to launch into his story just then, that was for sure. Christina needed her sleep.

"Great. I'll be finished around eight, and then maybe we can go to breakfast," Christina replied.

"Sounds good," Parker said. "Sleep tight."

Parker sprawled on his bed, staring at the ceiling and wishing he could go to sleep. Instead he endlessly relived the events of the day. For a while he imagined himself stomping over to Townsend Acres and telling his dad off. That, of course, would solve nothing. His dad would pretend to look mystified and then deny that he'd been trying to sidetrack Parker's plans to event. "And here I was, trying to help you by buying you two great eventing horses," Brad would say, feigning innocence. It would only add more problems to an already troubled family relationship. *Maybe Christina can give me some advice tomorrow,* Parker thought. And after a while he finally drifted off to sleep.

The next morning Parker woke later than he had intended to. He threw on some clothes, slipped quietly through the Nelsons' darkened house, and went out to his truck. Driving toward Whitebrook, he cheered slightly at the sight of the fading morning mist. He rolled down his window and sucked in deep breaths of air. It was going to be another sweltering summer day. Though he longed to be in England, he still felt a deep connection to his home in Kentucky. Never did he love his home state so much as in the early morning.

Parker pulled into Whitebrook's driveway and parked in the stable area. Though it was early, the breeding and training farm run by Christina's parents, Ashleigh Griffen and Mike Reese, was alive with activity. It wasn't as big a farm as Townsend Acres, and it certainly wasn't as luxurious, but it was clean and well run—impressive in its own way.

The most important thing about Whitebrook, Parker thought for the thousandth time, *is that it has heart.* The horses there were happy, and the people who worked there were, too.

Parker's eyes swept over Whitebrook's neatly kept grounds as he walked toward the main buildings. Approaching the training barn, he could see Dani Martens and several other grooms readying horses for their morning workouts.

"Good morning, Dani," he said.

Dani raised an eyebrow when she saw Parker. "Hi. What are you doing here? I thought you were off to the land of Shakespeare," she called out as she placed a postage-stamp-size exercise saddle on a bay filly's back. The filly did a little toe dance, and Dani laughed

73

at her antics. "Stop it, you big baby," she scolded, her attention diverted from Parker.

Parker kept walking. "I was, but I've been star-cross'd," he quipped, snagging part of one of the Bard's lines from *Romeo and Juliet.*

"Ah. Double, double toil and trouble?" said Dani knowingly, quoting *Macbeth.*

Parker grinned. "Yeah, something like that," he called back.

Approaching the training oval, he could see several horses breezing along, and his eyes searched for Christina.

"There she is," he said aloud. Just seeing her made his spirits lift.

Okay, so being delayed isn't all bad, Parker told himself. *I get to spend some time with Christina that I hadn't thought I would.*

Hurrying, Parker walked over to the rail next to Ian McLean, Whitebrook's head trainer, who was clocking Christina with a stopwatch that was dangling around his neck. Peering at the lanky colt she was riding, Parker racked his brain but found he couldn't place him. With over fifty horses on the place, that wasn't surprising.

"Who is Christina riding?" Parker asked Ian.

His eyes never leaving the track, Ian said, "His

name's Warlord. Arrived here a few weeks ago. A late bloomer, but he's got some of the same blood as War Emblem."

Parker frowned. "War Emblem?" he repeated, puzzled.

"Bob Baffert trained him. Eclipse winner," Ian said, referring to the coveted award the racing world bestowed on its greats. "This colt has some of War Emblem's firepower, that's for sure. But we've got to tap it."

Parker watched closer, studying the colt's fluid motion and outstretched head. Although he wasn't a die-hard racing fan, he still appreciated a good racehorse when he saw one.

"Let him out," Ian said, almost to himself, while Christina shot around the turn, expertly letting the reins thread through her fingers.

Parker watched as Christina flattened herself low onto the colt's withers, her hands kneading along the colt's neck. Once she gave him all the rein he needed, he opened up, shooting forward in response. Now Christina was a blur, but Parker could imagine the exhilaration she must be feeling as she rode past the black-and-white mile marker.

She loves racing as much as I love eventing, Parker thought, smiling. It was hardly the first time he had

had such a thought, but it didn't matter. He still felt how strongly sharing such similar passions for their sports drew them together.

But Christina is out there right now pursuing her passion, and here I am—sidelined, he thought remembering again why he was there.

After Christina slowed the colt and turned toward the gap to dismount, she climbed down from the saddle and handed the reins over to Dani. As Christina approached, Parker's heart skipped a beat. When she noticed him, her face lit up, and he smiled in response.

Ian scribbled a note onto his clipboard. "Nice ride, Chris," he commented. "Warlord showed some of his colors this morning, and that was because of you."

"Thanks," Christina replied with a smile, removing her helmet. She looked to check the time that Ian had jotted down. Then, glancing toward the track, where another colt was breezing, she asked, "Are you sure you don't want me to ride any more for you?"

"No, but thanks for helping me out this morning," Ian replied. "Now run along and say hello to this boyfriend of yours."

"I sure will. See you later, Ian," she said happily.

Walking over to Parker, she smoothed back a lock of his hair. "I've been told to say hello to you," she teased.

Parker hugged her and kissed her cheek lightly,

76

taking in the sensation of having her in his arms again.

"It sure is good to see you," Parker said, his voice shaking with emotion.

"I still can't believe you're here," Christina said. "When we said good-bye at Belmont, I was sure I wouldn't see you for at least a couple of months."

"Yeah, that's what I thought, too," Parker admitted.

Christina squeezed his hand. "Well, I'm thrilled you're here. But I know you well enough to know you're probably not thrilled to be here."

"Oh, I'm happy to see you, too, that's for sure," Parker assured her quickly. "But I've got to admit, I wish I were back in England right now."

Picturing Foxy's lovely head and deep, wise eyes, he felt his throat tighten. He ought to be on her back right now, skimming over the fields at Kempton Park, his eyes firmly fixed on the competition at Burghley.

"So then in the end I missed my plane, and I can't catch another for two more days," Parker said, concluding his story. He and Christina were sitting in Brewed Attitude, a new coffeehouse that had opened up a few weeks earlier.

They were settled on a comfy, overstuffed couch near the back entrance, away from most of the other patrons. Parker hadn't wanted anyone to overhear him. Lexington was a pretty big place, but the horse world within it was pretty small. Parker knew that most people were very aware of who his parents were. The last thing he wanted was for someone to report back to Brad what Parker had been saying.

Christina looked at Parker, her eyes full of sympathy. "What a completely rotten situation," she said, drumming her fingers against her coffee cup. "Those horses must be something pretty special if they could make you forget everything else."

Parker nodded. "Oh, they are, all right," he replied. "When I first saw them at Rolex, my eyes bugged right out of my head. I saw them being jumped and schooled in the dressage ring one afternoon, and their talent blew me away. They're kind of green, but wow. With a little time and experience, they'll be standouts."

Christina smiled. "Well, no one can say your dad doesn't have an eye for good horses," she said.

"And he certainly gets his money's worth when he buys one," Parker shot back.

"He didn't say that there were strings attached to the horses. Maybe for once he just wanted to give you a gift."

"Some gift! Those horses must have cost the moon," Parker said, stirring his café mocha.

"Okay, so a really *big* gift. Two of them." Christina

smirked. "Maybe now that the Triple Crown's over, he's started thinking about other things. Maybe he feels guilty that he's been such a jerk all these years. You're sure he's up to something?"

Parker snorted. "Come on. Have you ever known my dad *not* to be up to something?"

Christina tilted her head and laughed. "No," she admitted. "But in this case, what does he have to gain?"

"Me, right in the palm of his hand. That's what," Parker replied. "If I said yes, he'd start telling me what to do with them. Pretty soon he'd start putting the squeeze on me to stop eventing and insist that I help him run Townsend Acres. You know the story by now."

Christina pursed her lips thoughtfully. "You could talk with him some more and tell him that if he really means it, if there aren't any strings attached, you'd be happy to accept the horses."

Parker ran his finger around the rim of his cup. "You make it sound easy," he said softly.

"Well, I just hate to see you pass up something like this," Christina exclaimed. "I mean, I know it's out of character for your dad, but maybe just this once he really means exactly what he says. And he *did* say there were no strings attached. So . . ."

Just then Parker's cell phone rang. "Now who could this be?" Parker muttered, annoyed at the interruption. He rolled his eyes in apology as he answered it.

"Parker?" It was his mom.

"Good morning, Mother," he said.

"Oh, Parker, it's a horrible morning. Are you still in the United States? You have to come home right away!" Lavinia burst out hysterically.

Parker sat upright and clutched the phone. "Yes, I'm still here. Why? What happened?"

Lavinia burst into sobs. "It's your father. King's Ransom ran over him last night on his way back to the stallion barn. Get over here right away—that is, if you care at *all*!"

"Why didn't you call me last night?" Parker exclaimed, feeling the blood drain from his face.

"How could we think of *you* at a time like that?" his mother replied, cutting Parker to the quick.

"I'll be there," Parker mumbled as he pressed the end button on his phone.

"What's going on?" Christina asked, eyes huge.

"My father," Parker choked out. "There's been an accident. I've got to get home!"

7

"HELLO?" PARKER CALLED AS HE CHARGED THROUGH THE
door of the manor house.

The moment Parker's feet hit the marble floor in
the entryway, he sensed the hush that had permeated
the air. The servants he encountered barely acknowl-
edged him and hurried about their business silently.
Connie looked at Parker with a frightened expression
and pointed upstairs toward his parents' room.

As Parker bolted up the vast staircase, he found his
feelings were swirling within him like a stormy sea.
Just an hour earlier he'd been raging against his dad
for tripping him up. Now his stomach was tight with
worry and guilt. It was too much to take in, and Parker
had trouble catching his breath.

A stallion had run over his father? Instantly his mind flashed back to a story that was legendary in the racing world. The son of Wayne Lukas, one of the most famous trainers in racing history, had been run over by a two-year-old colt named Tabasco Cat. That story had turned out all right in the end, with Jeff recovering. Tabasco Cat, of course, had gone on to win two legs of the Triple Crown. But before Jeff got better, he'd lain in a deep coma for months.

Shuddering, Parker tried to shove that story to the back of his mind. Surely his dad's situation wasn't the same. Wouldn't his mother have told him? Wouldn't his dad still be in the hospital?

Dad's going to be okay, Parker assured himself.

Lavinia met him at the top of the stairs. Usually her face was a mask of composed disdain, but now it was white and drawn. Her blond hair, usually perfectly groomed, was thrown back as if she'd run her fingers through it one too many times.

"What took you so long?" she said in a brittle voice.

"I came as quickly as I could," he replied with forced calmness.

"Well, you're too late," Lavinia snapped. "He was calling for you, but the nurse just gave him his pain medication, and he won't be in any condition to see you now."

82

Parker stood on the top step, momentarily taken aback. "What happened?" he asked.

Lavinia twirled the diamond bracelet on her thin wrist in agitation. "It was too horrible," she said. "I don't want to talk about it."

"Mother, I need to know," Parker persisted.

Just then a uniformed nurse appeared down the hall. "Mrs. Townsend, I'd like to speak with you," she said.

Lavinia glanced at Parker. "Your father will be awake in a while, and he'll want to see you. I'll let you know when he's ready," she said dismissively as she turned toward the nurse.

Nodding, Parker did an about-face and walked back down the stairs. He felt like a Ping-Pong ball being batted back and forth: *Go here. Leave now. Come back.* And he still had no idea what had happened!

Without thinking about where he was going, Parker found himself headed back toward the paddock where Fanfaer and Black Hawke had been turned out the day before. As he approached the white fence, he saw that the paddock was empty.

Where did they go? Parker wondered.

"Parker," came a voice from behind him.

Parker glanced over his shoulder. It was Jeff Gaines, the stable hand.

"Mr. Townsend told me this morning that if you stopped by, he wanted you to take out the two horses he just purchased," the hand said.

"He just got in some sort of accident, and he told you this?" Parker was dumbfounded.

"That's the word I got an hour ago," Gaines admitted.

Parker looked sharply at the stable hand. "Do *you* know what happened?" he asked.

Gaines looked away and appeared to be nervous. Parker knew why. Brad had always given the people he'd hired strict instructions never to discuss anything with outsiders, whether it was the press or farm visitors. "My business is no one's business," Parker had heard his dad telling his employees more than once.

Parker folded his arms across his chest. "I'm family, in case you didn't know." Then he added more quietly. "Look, I'll never tell anyone that you told me."

Gaines regarded him for a moment and apparently decided to trust him.

"It was just about feeding time. Mr. Townsend was arguing with the stallion manager about something when King's Ransom broke away from his handler and charged him," Gaines finally muttered reluctantly. "Ran right over him."

"That much I gathered," Parker said. "But how badly was he hurt?"

84

Gaines shook his head. "It didn't seem to be too bad. He was taken away in an ambulance, and all we know is that he came back to the house this morning accompanied by a couple of nurses," he replied.

Parker tried to make sense of this new information. If his father had been released, then it couldn't be *too* serious, could it? He felt himself relaxing a little bit.

"Fanfaer and Black Hawke are being readied for you," Gaines said, turning on his heel and walking toward the training barn.

No, Parker thought, but he followed Gaines as if in a stupor.

"You sure are beautiful," Parker said softly, stroking Black Hawke's velvety muzzle a few minutes later.

The black horse was standing in the crossties, whuffing Parker inquisitively. Parker laughed as the horse's trimmed whiskers tickled the top of his head. For a moment he closed his eyes and inhaled the sweet smell of horse and hay. Oh, how incredible it would be to own a horse like Black Hawke as well as his wonderful Foxy and Ozzie.

But that can never happen, Parker thought, drawing back reluctantly. "Well, big guy, I'm sure you'll make your new owner very proud," Parker said, stroking his shoulder.

At the sound of horseshoes ringing against the concrete, Parker turned. It was Fanfaer, being led by a stable hand, a young woman who looked to be about his age. Though she didn't say anything as she clipped the big bay into the crossties, Parker could see the admiration for the horse in her eyes.

"I'll go get your saddle," she said, glancing at Parker.

"No need, Emily," Parker said, reading her name tag. "I'm not riding."

Emily made no effort to mask her surprise. "You're seriously going to pass up a chance to ride horses like these?" The next moment she clapped her hand over her mouth. "Sorry. It's none of my business."

Parker smiled wearily. "Don't worry about it," he said. "Between you and me, it's killing me not to climb aboard, but it's just not possible."

Emily grinned back, understanding shooting between the two of them, but she made no comment.

Wants to keep her job, Parker thought ruefully, heading up the barn aisle. He might as well wait at the house to see his dad instead of being led astray at the barn and allowing himself to fall further in love with Fanfaer and Black Hawke.

Parker tried not to think about the two horses as he sat in the front room waiting for the summons from his father. Looking around at the formal living room, his eye rested on the shimmering silk curtains at the tall windows and the delicate ornaments on the carved mantel of the fireplace. He wished himself thousands of miles away. This room brought back too many unhappy memories of the many society parties held within its walls. And when there hadn't been parties there, Parker's parents had been off at other parties around Lexington, leaving him by himself to rattle around in the big house, wishing for a real family.

How he would love to be galloping across Kempton Park on Foxy just then. He'd give anything to feel the wind rush against him as he analyzed an upcoming fence and figured out the best angle for his approach. Parker shifted in his chair and sighed. Instead he was sitting on his rear on an uncomfortable damask-covered chair, worried about his father while despising him at the same time. He tried to force himself to concentrate on other, less upsetting topics. He let his mind sink into a daydream about being back in England.

"Your father will see you."

At the sound of his mother's voice, Parker's eyes flew open. He had fallen into a light sleep leaning against the wood-paneled wall. Rubbing his neck, he jumped up.

"I don't know how you can sleep at a time like this, with your father lying there in pain," Lavinia said accusingly as she motioned him to follow her upstairs.

Walking up the stairs, Parker glared at his mother's thin back.

"That's not fair," he muttered. It wasn't because he wasn't concerned. It was simply because he was exhausted.

"Now, I don't want you to be shocked at what you see," Lavinia advised Parker as they stopped outside the bedroom door, where a uniformed male nurse was stationed.

"Tell me the truth. How bad is he?" Parker asked, searching his mother's face as the nurse stood up.

Lavinia sighed dramatically and put her manicured hand over her heart. Big tears welled up in her eyes. "When I first saw him in the hospital, I thought for sure we—we were going to lose him," she whispered.

Parker stepped back and let his mouth drop open. He had had no idea that things were that bad.

"Don't worry," Lavinia added, her lip quivering. "The doctors have hope that maybe, just maybe, he'll pull through okay."

Swallowing hard, Parker steeled himself before opening the door.

When Parker entered the room, he had to let his

eyes adjust for a few seconds to the dimness. There was one low light switched on in the opposite corner of the bedroom, but the area surrounding the large mahogany four-poster bed was very dark.

"He can't stand the light right now. It makes his headache worse," Lavinia whispered when she saw Parker's questioning look. "Go on now. He's awake."

With that, Lavinia stepped out of the room, and Parker approached his father's bedside. As his eyes grew more accustomed to the semidarkness, he could see that his father's face was ghostly pale against the white pillows placed behind his head. Brad's nose was covered with a white bandage, his cheek was black and bruised, and his left eye was swollen shut. "You came," Brad exclaimed weakly, feebly holding out the arm that was in a sling. He winced as he did so and sucked in his breath loudly.

"Of course I did," Parker said, trying not to look horrified. He had never seen his dad look anything but sure and in command. But at the moment Brad looked shrunken, tired, and defeated. It suddenly occurred to Parker that Brad seemed surprised that he had come to see him.

Does my dad think that I'm such a jerk I wouldn't dash right over when he'd just been in an accident? Parker was shocked at the thought. True, he and his father had never been on the best of terms, but looking at him now, Parker found himself feeling horribly guilty.

"Let this be a lesson to you," Brad said, gesturing for Parker to sit in a nearby chair. "Whenever a twelve-hundred-pound stallion charges toward you, get out of the way immediately." He smiled wanly at his joke and winced again.

Parker tried to grin in response, but he found he couldn't. Instead he nodded. "How did it happen?"

Brad closed the one eye that Parker could see, and a spasm of pain crossed his face. "That fool of a stable hand led Ransom right by me, and he let the stud chain go slack. That's all the son of a gun needed. The next minute he broke free of his handler and tore away. I happened to be standing in the wrong place at the wrong time. No warning. Wham!"

"I'm sorry, Dad," Parker said gently.

Brad opened his eye again and lifted one corner of his mouth. "Well, for a few moments there it looked as though you might be inheriting Townsend Acres sooner than either of us had expected."

Parker sucked in his breath. "Dad!" he said. "Don't talk like that!"

Brad sighed. "Well, let's not kid ourselves," he said. "I'm sure you've thought about how things would be if something happened to me."

"No, I really haven't," Parker replied honestly.

"Well, I hadn't, either," Brad went on. "But last night at the hospital it occurred to me that it was high time both of us thought about that. It's not easy for a man to face that he might not be around forever, but once King's Ransom forced the issue, I knew it was time you and I talked."

Parker was silent for a moment. Finally he blurted out, "But there's still Mom."

Brad shook his head. "Your mother isn't cut out to run a farm. You and I both know that," he said.

Parker arched a brow. If there was one thing he knew about his mother, it was that she could run anything she wanted to. Lavinia might not do so in a caring way, but she was as tough as nails underneath her ladylike exterior. She definitely was equipped to step in and take over the running of the farm. "Of course she could," Parker countered.

"Be that as it may," Brad replied evenly, his voice surprisingly stronger, "she and I have talked, and we both agree that the running of the farm will fall to you."

Parker shook his head. "But I've told you again and again—"

Brad held up his good hand. "Say no more. I know you want to ride in the Olympics, and I'm prepared to help you do that. You saw the horses I bought for you.

Can you doubt that I'm serious about helping you?"

"Well—" Parker began, but his dad cut him off again.

"Those pretty boys cost me a fortune, let me tell you."

"I know they did," Parker replied meekly. "Everyone says they're Olympic caliber."

"But once you've ridden in the Olympics, you'll see that there's more than hauling about, jumping over a few toppled trees. It'll be time to come home and look your future squarely in the eye. It's here, at Townsend Acres," Brad commanded.

Seeing Parker's look, Brad charged on, but in a softer tone. "I'll teach you everything I know," he said. "We'll run the place side by side, me giving you the tricks of the trade you couldn't get from anyone else. It may take years before you learn my way, but one day you'll thank me for teaching you something more important than that eventing foolishness."

Parker looked at his father, who now fell back against his pillows, his energy spent. Standing up, Parker gritted his teeth. "It's not foolishness," Parker said, trying to control his sudden fierce anger. "And it won't be over when I ride in the Olympics. There's still a lot more I want to do with eventing after the Olympics. That's just the beginning."

"After the Olympics? What else is there to do?"

Brad paused, then went on. "You mean you seriously plan to go risk your neck over those ridiculous fences in every run-down country in Europe?"

Parker nodded.

Brad sighed. "Do you want to spend your life living out of motels, starting all kinds of miserable horses like that fleabag Ozzie of yours, hoping that maybe you'll find one that has an ounce of talent? Just how long do you think you could sustain the life of an impoverished rider? Better get used to scraping for every miserable cent."

"I don't need to be rich to be happy," Parker growled, unable to control his anger anymore. How dare his dad call Ozzie a fleabag!

A muscle in Brad's jaw twitched. "Who says being rich is about being happy?" he asked. "Being rich is what enables you to pull together a state-of-the-art medical facility and hire top veterinarians like James Dalton to save down-on-their-luck horses like Image."

Parker's head snapped up. He couldn't believe that his dad was throwing it in his face that he had saved Melanie's horse's life.

"That's a low blow, Dad," Parker spat coldly.

Brad nodded. "The truth hurts, doesn't it? Money buys the best—people, technology, and, yeah, the finer things in life. Fine horses, premier breeding farms like Townsend Acres."

"I don't need the finer things in life," Parker countered.

"Yeah, you do, but you're only eighteen, and you just don't know it," Brad persisted.

"I'm not you, Dad," Parker practically shouted. As soon as the words left his mouth, Parker felt like a total jerk. He was shouting at a man who had just come home from the hospital. A man who, for whatever reason, had arranged it so that Image was now recovering happily instead of being a sad Kentucky Derby legend and a mere memory.

Still, none of this changed the fact that his father, as usual, was doing everything within his power to force Parker to bend to his wishes.

"Look, Dad," Parker went on more softly. "I'm sure this accident has been awful for you. But nothing has changed. I need to stay on my path. Townsend Acres is your dream—not mine."

Brad fixed him with a hard look. "Stay home. Don't go back to England."

Parker met his gaze. "I can't do that."

Brad's eye narrowed. "You're ungrateful and shortsighted," he snapped. "You're passing up the chance of a lifetime."

Parker stood there for a moment, conflict raging inside him. Finding he couldn't put his feelings into words, he leaned over to touch his father's shoulder.

Brad pulled away and picked up the cordless telephone. He waved his good hand dismissively, like a king who was tired of his courtier.

"There are other ways to look at it," Parker said, his voice rising in spite of his effort to speak calmly.

Feeling sick, angry, and sad, Parker turned and strode out of the room.

As he started down the hallway he heard Brad bellow into the phone, "Turner! I want you to sell those two miserable meatballs I just bought. . . . Yeah, you heard right! I want them off this property *now*!"

8

HOW COULD I HAVE DONE THAT? PARKER ASKED HIMSELF, stepping onto the front porch of the manor house. With his dad lying there battered and bruised from a bad accident, he had just told him off and stormed out.

"What kind of a son am I?" Parker muttered. Leaning against a massive Doric column, Parker tried to collect his thoughts. Maybe he needed to go back inside and try to reason with his dad one more time. Maybe he ought to apologize.

Shaking his head, he realized that would never do. "I can't apologize. What else *could* I have done? My dad was trying to ruin my life!" he mumbled in a daze. "He was trying to cut me off from what I love, and tie me down to Townsend Acres."

Straightening, Parker lifted his chin. His eyes swept over the vast panorama that was Townsend Acres. In the summer sun it looked glorious. It seemed to go on forever. As far as he could see, there were acres of green pastures, fabulous buildings and facilities, horses and more horses. Off in the distance there was even a huge lake. Parker bit his lip as he studied the sparkling water.

Diamonds, Parker thought, watching the sunlight play off the water. When it came to Kentucky horse farms, there was no doubt that this place was just that—a diamond. Glittering, beckoning, maybe. But also cold. And very, very hard.

Dad was just trying to give me something wonderful, he thought, his emotions still churning. *Is there anything wrong with that?*

"Was I crazy to turn him down?" he said aloud, walking slowly toward his truck.

Looking around one last time, Parker climbed into the cab and started down the long drive.

Parker asked himself the same questions over and over as he sped toward Whisperwood. *How many people are lucky enough to have a world-class breeding and training operation handed to them on a silver platter? Am I being too closed-minded about this? I've never given it a chance. Maybe I could get used to running a racing farm.*

While Parker drove, he pictured himself trying to

97

fit into the life his father had carved out for him. He would have ridden in the Olympics already. He would feel differently about eventing after his Olympic dream had become a reality. He would focus his energy and learn more about running a racehorse operation. And maybe his desire to rip across a cross-country course could be pushed into the background.

Then another image popped into Parker's head: himself spending hours sitting in the barn office, poring over stud books and analyzing Thoroughbred bloodlines. Parker frowned. Before he knew it, he'd be a walking encyclopedia, talking about dosages, sires, dams, and progeny everywhere he went. *Talk about boring!*

And that would be just the beginning, of course. He'd have to promote his stallions by jetting around the world and hobnobbing with all the right people. He'd have to throw lavish parties and show up at other people's parties. That was how the game was played. It was one thing to decide to go to a party with pals. It was another thing entirely to be required to go to a party for one purpose—to wheel and deal, trying to convince everyone in the racing world that he had a lock on the next big winner. The world of racing was fast-paced and high-stakes—and it left no time for devoting himself to the sport he loved with all his heart.

Could I really be happy running an operation like Townsend Acres for the rest of my life? No. Definitely not, Parker concluded as he turned into the driveway at Whisperwood. Even if he could convince himself to become interested in racing, he could never run a farm the way Brad did. Where Parker cared deeply about horses and their well-being, his father cared only about power and fame and money. Brad would do whatever it took to grab the advantage, even if it meant using training methods that bordered on cruelty.

Shuddering, Parker thought back to when Star had been in training at Townsend Acres under Ralph Dunkirk, the head trainer. A sensitive horse used to gentle handling, Star had undergone a personality transformation under Ralph's harsh treatment. And Ralph's harshness had been carried out under Brad's orders.

No, I could never be part of an operation like that, Parker concluded. He parked his truck and climbed out of the cab.

But if I did the right thing, then why do I feel so bad?

Walking toward the barn, Parker continued replaying the day in his mind, and his thoughts locked onto the last thing he'd heard his dad say as he had walked out: *Sell those two miserable meatballs.*

That's what his dad had called Black Hawke and Fanfaer—*meatballs!* They were two of the most spectacular horses on earth. And it was quite possible that at this very moment they were being loaded into a van to be shipped off to a sales barn or some run-down auction house. Parker knew his dad was angry enough at him that for once he wouldn't care about losing money on the horses. He'd sell them off as quickly as he could just to have them out of the way. Just to punish Parker.

Anyone could pick up those two incredible horses—even someone who'd overjump them and push them beyond their limits.

The thought made Parker sick, and he stopped for a moment. He couldn't walk into the barn the way he was feeling just then. His students were great, horse-loving kids. They didn't need to be brought down by his long face and his problems. He took a deep breath to calm himself.

Plastering on a smile, Parker finally stepped into the barn's dimly lit interior, where several students were readying their horses for a lesson. Normally the sound of their laughter and chatter would brighten Parker's spirits. But not that day.

"Hey, Parker, you're back," called out Justin, whose horse, Bouncer, was standing tacked up in the crossties. "I thought you were gone."

Penny emerged from the tack room carrying her crop. "Did you come back to give us our lesson today?"

Parker smiled in spite of his black mood and ruffled her hair. "No, Blaine is. I'm technically not supposed to be here," he said. *I'm supposed to be in England schooling my horses.*

Penny pushed her mouth into a pout. "We miss you," she said. "We want *you* to give us our lessons."

Parker bit his lip. The last thing he wanted to do just then was give anyone lessons on any subject. But Penny's earnest face made him reconsider. Maybe he didn't know anything about normal families, but at least he knew how to take care of horses. Maybe if he helped out in some small way, he wouldn't feel like such a loser.

"All right, then. You asked for it. How about I give you a lesson right now?" Parker said, walking over to Chili and inspecting him. Frowning, he reached over to unbuckle a twisted throatlatch on Chili's bridle. Running his hands over Chili's thick mane, he pulled out several pieces of bedding.

"You wouldn't show up at school wearing pajamas, would you? Same thing. Now, did you pick out his hooves thoroughly?" Parker asked Penny on a hunch.

The little girl ducked her head guiltily. "I—uh—forgot," she admitted.

Parker pulled out his folding hoof pick and handed it to her. "Never, never take shortcuts when it comes to horses," he said automatically. How many times had he said that exact phrase to his students?

While Penny busied herself with Chili's feet, Parker walked over and inspected the other students' horses. He found that Justin had forgotten to put on Bouncer's protective boots and that Kelsey had put the wrong bridle on Mr. Chips.

"It looks like you guys are slipping a little in the detail department," Parker said gently. "Horsemanship is more about horse care than riding. I'm sure Blaine tells you that till he's blue in the face."

Just then Blaine walked in. He grinned as he saw Parker. "You're right about the blue-in-the-face part," he said. Winking at the kids, he added in a stage whisper, "Good thing he decided to hang around here a few days so he can keep an eye on you barn rats."

Parker nodded. "Yeah," he said, going along with the joke and adjusting Justin's girth. "It's a hassle changing plans just to nag you all, but it's worth it."

After he watched the students lead their horses out toward the ring behind Blaine, Parker turned and wandered over to the paddock where one of Tor's prize prospects, Nighthawk, was grazing. The big colt ambled over to the white fence, and Parker stroked his nose absently, idly wondering if Nighthawk also had Welton blood in him, like Black Hawke did.

What was he doing here killing time with other

people's horses when he had his own to worry about? Every day that he wasn't there training them put him one day further from riding in the Olympics. Yet England seemed very far away right now. The main thought filling his head was of how his father had tried to take advantage of Parker's concern about his injury, and how two innocent horses were going to pay the price.

That evening Parker picked up Christina and took her to dinner at Tino's, their favorite local Mexican restaurant. It was their last night together. Christina was leaving in the morning to go back to Belmont. Parker filled Christina in on Brad's accident and then urged her to tell him about Star and her plans once she returned to the racetrack in New York.

But Christina shook her head. "First I want you to tell me what *else* is going on. If your dad is really doing all right, then why do you seem so upset? There's something more you're not telling me, right?"

Nodding, Parker pushed the food around on his plate and told Christina about the disastrous interview with his father.

"So he *did* buy the horses to rope you in," Christina exclaimed. "And to think that I was even entertaining the thought that for once he was being a nice guy."

"All I can think of is those poor horses," Parker finished helplessly. "I wish there were something I could do."

Christina reached across the table to take Parker's hand. Her eyes were troubled. "I'm so sorry," she said softly.

Parker intertwined his fingers with hers and managed a half smile. "Me too," he muttered. "But as usual, my dad holds all the cards."

"Well, maybe the horses will still somehow end up getting good homes," she said, trying to boost his spirits.

"Or maybe not," Parker replied darkly.

Christina drummed her fingers on the table. "Why not make sure they do?" she asked, excitement creeping into her voice.

"How?" Parker was puzzled.

Christina's eyes lit up. "Find out where your dad's taking them. Then tip off some of your rich eventing friends. Maybe they'll want to buy one or both."

"I have eventing friends, but I don't have any *rich* friends," Parker replied.

"Sure you do," she said. "Think. *Think*."

"I *am* thinking," Parker shot back.

Christina twisted a lock of her reddish brown hair. "How about David Breen? Didn't you say he was rolling in it? Doesn't he live around here somewhere?"

"David? He's rich, all right, but he had the chance once before to buy the horses, and he passed. They were probably too expensive even for him."

"If your dad's looking to unload them in a hurry, he'll have to take a price drop. Then David might be able to afford them," Christina pointed out.

Parker nodded slowly. Christina was right. But there was one other problem. "David's one of my competitors," he said. "Why give him a crack at horses that could beat the pants off me one day?"

"Because you're a true horseman," Christina said. "I know you. A horse's well-being always comes first with you, even before competition."

Parker looked at her and smiled. "You know what? You're right, Reese," he said, taking her hand. "And Connie's right. You *do* help me see things straight."

"Glad to be of help," Christina tossed back playfully.

"Now here's the next problem," Parker went on. "I have no idea which crummy auction house the horses will end up at. There's a zillion of 'em around here."

Christina grinned. "You can find out, can't you?"

"I'm not sure," Parker confessed. "You know my dad. He can be pretty sneaky when he wants to."

Christina nodded. "Yeah, but it's nothing you can't handle. Time to do a little detective work. I think you're up to it, don't you?"

105

When Parker hesitated, she added, "The Parker Townsend I know wouldn't let a little thing like that stop him!"

Parker looked at her challenging stare and jumped up.

"Let's go!" he cried, blood coursing through him. "We don't have time to waste!"

9

"WELL, SO MUCH FOR GETTING DAVID BREEN TO BUY THE horses," Parker muttered.

It was several hours later, and Parker was up in his room, looking moodily out the window over Whisperwood's darkened fields. After he'd dropped Christina off at Whitebrook, he had gone back to Townsend Acres and managed to pry the name of the auction house out of Jeff Gaines. Jeff hadn't wanted to tell him, but Parker had been at his persuasive best, and finally Jeff had cracked.

Afterward he'd put in a call to David Breen. Unfortunately, one of David's efficient staffers had answered the phone, saying that David was unavailable and that she would be glad to take a message. The more Parker had begged the staffer to put the call through, the more she repeated her statement. And then Parker *did* try to leave a message that David should call him back, but he could tell from the staffer's tone that she probably wasn't going to give the message to David. She probably thought Parker was just another crackpot. Though Parker was furious at the roadblock, he couldn't help but understand. Famous riders like David got calls all the time—from nutcases, overzealous fans, and people trying to sell them things.

"Yeah, like the next big horse," Parker had muttered with a sigh as he hung up.

I'm right back where I started, Parker thought now. *I can't get hold of David. Who else could afford these horses?*

Pacing around his room, he mentally reviewed his list of eventing friends. Immediately he crossed Lyssa Hynde off the list. She didn't have the money, and besides, now that she'd been picked up for the Olympic team, she was getting all kinds of offers for great horses to ride. Anyway, she was training in New Jersey and couldn't get down to Kentucky in time to buy the horses even if she was in a position to buy.

No, that left only David.

I've got to do something, Parker thought. Suddenly he slapped the side of his head. What was he thinking? He didn't need to wait for the staffer to pass along the phone message. He could just drive to David's farm. It was on the outskirts of Lexington. Parker had been to his place once, a long time ago, for a clinic.

I bet I remember the way, Parker thought, throwing on his University of Kentucky sweatshirt and dashing out into the night to climb into his truck.

A few minutes later he was cruising down the highway. With the radio blaring, Parker felt his mood improve. The moon was full, and he had no trouble finding his way to David's place.

When he pulled into the driveway, he was surprised to see that the farm had a guarded gatehouse, just as Townsend Acres did.

That's funny—I don't remember this, Parker thought, driving slowly up to the gatehouse. *I guess it makes sense. Now that David's big-time, it's smart to think about security, like any racing stable would.*

"Name, please, sir," said the guard.

"Parker Townsend to see David Breen," Parker called back.

The guard looked puzzled. He glanced at a clipboard. "I don't see your name here. Is he expecting you?"

"Uh, no," Parker admitted. "I tried to call but couldn't get through. Can you call up to the house?"

The guard nodded. "I'm afraid that's impossible."

"Is David home?" Parker pressed.

The guard didn't answer.

109

He probably thinks I'm a demented fan or something, coming for an autograph or to steal a piece of his horse's mane! Parker realized.

"Look, I'm not a fan. I'm a friend of his," Parker said, frustration creeping into his voice. "He and I are competitors on the eventing circuit together."

The guard looked at him. "Competitors, huh?" His eyes were full of suspicion.

Parker ran his fingers through his hair in frustration. "I haven't come here to sabotage his horses, if that's what you're thinking. I need to tell him something very important," he said.

"I'm afraid that's impossible. You're welcome to leave the message with me, and I'll deliver it," the guard replied.

No, Parker decided instantly. That wouldn't do. How did he know that the information wouldn't somehow get back to his dad?

Parker backed up his truck and, banging his fist on the steering wheel, started down the road toward home. Seconds later, however, he pulled up. He was going to tell David about the horses if it killed him.

But how?

I'll have to sneak onto the place, he decided. *I'll climb a fence or something.*

The moon was full, and Parker found he could see pretty well. Eyeing the tall hedge bordering the road,

Parker decided he could probably climb it. He glanced back and saw that the gatehouse was set back from the road. *The guard can't see me over here.*

Shutting off the truck's engine, Parker pulled up the parking brake and climbed out.

I hope there's no electric fence behind that hedge.

Gingerly Parker pulled back some of the bushy hedge and peered around. No sign of a fence.

Well, here goes. Parker Townsend storms Fort Breen.

With that, Parker started scaling the hedge. Immediately he felt himself being jabbed and scratched. Though he was wearing a thick sweatshirt, it offered little protection against the sharp branches. In a minute, though, he was over the top. Landing with a thud onto some hard ground, Parker looked around and realized he was in a pasture. The full moon gave him a clear view of a barn up ahead, and Parker darted across the pasture toward it.

Walking up to the barn, Parker could hear the rustling of horses in their bedding and the occasional sound of a whinny. He froze as he heard someone singing along to a radio.

I'm dead meat if anyone sees me, Parker thought, his heart thumping wildly in his chest. He moved on carefully, darting behind the poplar trees dotting the fields, trying to be as silent as possible.

Where's the main house? Parker wondered, trying to

111

get his bearings. Soon he was able to make out the shadowy outline of a low ranch-style house to the left of the barn.

That's it! Parker thought, picking up his pace and walking in that direction. Nervously he glanced over his shoulder, hoping that no one had spotted him. His imagination kicked into overdrive, and he started picturing himself being thrown into jail for trespassing. He imagined his mother having to come to the local jail to pick him up, and despite his nervousness, he had to suppress a smile. Lavinia would absolutely flip out.

Even worse, Parker thought, sobering, everyone in Lexington would know about it in no time. Brad Townsend was enough of a name in the area that a story about his son being arrested would be picked up by every news wire around.

Swallowing hard, Parker pictured the headline in the next day's local newspaper: *Noted Trainer's Son Seized Trespassing at Lexington Farm.*

Stop freaking yourself out, Parker admonished himself. *You're not going to get caught.*

But as he approached the house, he began to have more second thoughts. Even if he wasn't spotted and arrested, what would an eventing celebrity such as David Breen think about Parker Townsend, Olympic wanna-be, sneaking up to his house like a thief in the night with a crazy story about some cheap horses?

Sure, you wanted to tip me off about some fabulous horses, Parker could hear David saying sarcastically. Parker remembered a time a few years before when he and David had teamed up at an after-event party and had done an impromptu skit about two seedy horse traders trying to rip each other off. Parker had been in top form that night, and David had played off him perfectly. The crowd had laughed uproariously at their performance. Afterward David had joked, "If you ever give up eventing, you'd make a good horse trader, Townsend. You could talk the hind leg off a donkey."

He's going to think I'm pulling his leg in a repeat performance of our skit. Or worse, he'll think I'm some sort of nutcase, Parker thought grimly.

That was a chance he would have to take.

Tripping over a patch of uneven ground, Parker felt pain shoot up his leg. He'd twisted his ankle. He stopped for a few seconds to massage it, then walked on.

Suddenly he heard a low growl from behind him, and his blood froze. A guard dog? Some sort of vicious Doberman or Rottweiler specially trained to rip off the arms of anyone who dared to trespass or hurt the horses?

Turning around slowly at the sound, Parker was relieved to see a small, curly-haired mutt. Thinking fast, Parker crouched and snapped his fingers, calling,

"Here, boy." The dog paused but growled again.

Catching sight of a stick at his feet, Parker bent down and picked it up. "Here, boy," he repeated. "Want to play throw the stick?"

Luckily, the dog wagged his tail and began wriggling with excitement. Running over to Parker, he proceeded to lick Parker's face lavishly before grabbing the stick.

"Some watchdog you are," Parker scolded, scratching the dog's ears after he tossed the stick and the dog had returned with it. "Big growl. No bite. But lucky for me."

The little dog escorted him companionably to the front porch of the main house, darting about and bringing him more sticks to throw.

"Sorry, little guy, I don't have time to play anymore now," Parker whispered. Standing at the front door, he rang the doorbell, peering into the darkened sidelights anxiously. A minute passed, and then another.

Oh, great—I've gone to all this trouble, and no one's even home.

Suddenly Parker felt a hysterical urge to laugh. What a loser he was! He'd ripped his clothes, twisted his ankle, risked getting caught—and it was all for nothing. David wasn't even there.

I'll leave him a note, Parker thought. But then he shook his head as he patted his jeans pockets. It had never occurred to him to bring a pen. *This just gets worse and worse, doesn't it?*

Suddenly Parker was seized with inspiration. It wasn't a great plan, but it would have to do.

Working feverishly, Parker licked his finger and wrote a message in the dirt on the window by the front door.

Wow, David's window washer certainly isn't doing a very good job. It will be a miracle if David reads this, but hey, I tried, Parker thought, suddenly exhausted beyond belief. Turning, Parker walked back the way he had come, stealthily passing by the barn, escorted all the way by David's dog.

"Bye, guy," Parker called as he climbed the hedge again. "Don't tell on me, okay?"

An hour later Parker was back at Whisperwood and was just drifting off to sleep when his cell phone rang, startling him. Groaning, he picked it up.

Now what? he thought. It was probably his mom demanding that he return and apologize or something. He didn't think he could take any more family theatrics.

He was relieved when he heard his grandfather's voice.

"Did I wake you, Parker?" Clay asked. "I always

forget what time it is in the States when I'm across the pond."

"Me too, but you didn't wake me," Parker replied. "Where are you, Grandfather?"

"Still in Ireland with some old friends," Clay replied. "I was planning to come down to the UK to visit and watch you school Foxy, but the Chillinghams informed me that you're still in Kentucky. I called to make sure everything was all right."

Parker was tempted to fill his grandfather in on everything, but he held back. Things had always been tense between Brad and Clay, and Parker didn't want to add to the discord. "Everything's primo," Parker replied in a voice that sounded fake even to him. "Just a little delay of game."

"Delay of game?" Clay asked. "What exactly does that mean? Last I checked, it's a little over a month till Burghley. Seems to me you ought to be preparing if you want to play in *that* game."

Parker sighed. As if he hadn't been thinking the same thing himself!

"Is that son of mine giving you grief again?" his grandfather asked.

For one crazy minute Parker was ready to blurt out the whole story and beg his grandfather to buy the two horses. That would solve everything. After all, his grandfather was so rich, the cost wouldn't matter at all to him. But Parker knew that Clay had already been more than kind to him, buying Foxy for him and sending him a ticket so that he could see Christina ride in the Triple Crown. No, Clay had done enough.

"No. Not really," Parker lied. "But Dad was hurt in an accident. I don't know if you knew."

"Accident?" Clay asked.

"One of his new stallions ran over him in the stable yard yesterday. He was at the hospital, but he's home now, resting."

"Hmmm," Clay said. "Can't be that bad if he was sent home."

"I don't know," Parker replied uncertainly. "He has a couple of nurses, and he looked kind of banged up."

But he's still strong enough to try to run my life as usual, Parker thought darkly.

"But your mother didn't say anything specific about his condition?" asked Clay.

"No," Parker replied. "But she seemed pretty worked up, the way she always is when something happens that wasn't part of one of her perfectly made plans."

"Well, I'll check in on your dad," Clay said. "Don't you worry about it too much. You know your father. He's a fighter, and he'll weather anything that's thrown his way."

"Yeah, I guess you're right," Parker agreed.

"Now, when are you going back to England?"

"Tomorrow. That's the soonest I could get a flight," Parker said quickly. "I—uh—missed my plane the other day, and this was the next flight I could get."

"Missed your plane, huh?"

"It was an accident," Parker exclaimed defensively.

"Well, you make sure you're on that plane tomorrow," Clay said seriously. "You've worked too hard to let your training slip now."

After Parker hung up the phone, he wondered again if he should have confided in his grandfather. Punching his pillow with frustration, he wished for the thousandth time that life wasn't always so complicated.

In a burst of energy, he jumped up and began stuffing his clothes into his duffel bag. He was going to go to the airport the next day bright and early. There was no way he was going to stay in Kentucky a minute longer than he had to!

10

"ON MY WAY—AT LAST," PARKER MUTTERED TO HIMSELF as he fastened his seat belt.

He had just planted himself in the economy section of the jumbo jet bound for London. Glancing hastily at his seatmate, he was relieved to see a rumpled-looking businessman buried in a thick paperback.

Good, thought Parker. He was in no mood to engage in five hours of small talk. He still was depressed about everything that had happened.

I told off my dad while he was lying injured in bed, and it's my fault that two amazing horses are going to be shipped off to rotten homes, Parker found himself thinking over and over.

While the plane rose into the air, Parker stared

straight ahead, trying not to let thoughts of Fanfaer and Black Hawke cloud his head. When he had left Whisperwood at first light, he had had no intention of stopping at Townsend Acres. But somehow his truck took a detour, and he found himself pulling into the stable yard just as a commercial rig showed up to haul Black Hawke and Fanfaer away.

"Are you sure you told me the right auction house?" Parker had asked Gaines, who had emerged from one of the barns, leading a blanketed Fanfaer toward the rig.

"Yeah," Gaines whispered, not meeting Parker's eyes. "You know I could get in big trouble if anyone found out I told you."

"I know that. Thank you," Parker whispered back.

Gaines led Fanfaer past, and within seconds another groom, Marcos, appeared leading Black Hawke. Like Fanfaer, Black Hawke was blanketed, his legs encased in thick shipping boots.

Black Hawke whinnied at Parker, and Parker patted him briefly on the nose.

"I'm so sorry, big guy," Parker whispered sadly before walking back to his truck.

All the way to the airport Parker had felt terrible.

But soon I'll be with Foxy and Ozzie, and everything will be all right again. Idly Parker picked up an old copy of *Practical Horseman* that he'd tossed into his backpack. Thumbing through the pages, he came across a spread that featured a shot of his friend David Breen taking a fence at Rolex. David was riding his big-boned chestnut, Intimidator. Smiling, Parker remembered what David had said about him: "All speed, no sense." A brave, bold eventer, Intimidator was getting along in years.

I sure hope David got my message, Parker thought, shutting the magazine and shoving it in the seat pocket in front of him. Though David was a fierce competitor, Parker had always admired the way he took care of his horses. He leaned back in his seat, trying to relax. He'd done all he could do.

By the time the plane landed in London, Parker had decided to put thoughts of his disastrous trip to Kentucky out of his head. Now was the time to look forward. He picked up his duffel from the baggage claim and headed outside. One thing he certainly *wasn't* looking forward to was that long bus ride to Kempton Hall, where he was staying. He definitely couldn't afford a taxi.

Bumping along in the ancient bus, Parker found himself growing more and more anxious to see his horses. Though Dalton was surely doing a good job looking after them, Parker knew there was no substi-

121

tute for riding them himself. It was the bond between horse and rider that made all the difference in a competitive event such as Burghley.

The evening shadows were stealing across the English landscape by the time the bus pulled up to the village square. Hoisting his duffel bag, Parker got off the bus and walked the remaining mile and a half to Kempton Hall. He knew he could have called someone to pick him up—Dalton's groom, Thomas, or maybe his friend Phillipa. But after hours of sitting on planes and in buses, Parker wanted nothing more than to stretch his long legs by walking. He began regretting that decision when rain started falling softly at first, then increasing in intensity. Soon his old paddock boots were soaked, squishing damply with every step.

Townsend, you are pathetic, Parker thought dismally as he sloshed along. *You're going to turn up at one of the finest homes in England looking like a drowned rat. You're every bit the poverty-stricken loser your old man expects you to be.*

Taking a deep breath as the Chillinghams' stately home came into view, Parker shifted his bag and continued up to the front door. The lights were low, and the house looked deserted.

Guess the Chillinghams aren't home, Parker thought, relieved that he wouldn't have to face anyone looking the way he did. Parker headed toward the side entrance, thinking that he could slip inside and change before anyone could see him in his drenched state. Then he would head over to the stables and look in on Foxy and Ozzie, who would be cozily tucked in their stalls for the night.

"It wasn't my fault!"

Parker's head snapped up as the side door sprang open and Fiona dashed out into the rain, followed by her shaggy Irish wolfhound, Wolfie. Wolfie sniffed at Parker in delight, but Fiona didn't notice him. She also seemed oblivious to the fact that she was barefoot and wearing her fuzzy bathrobe, which was now getting soaked by the rain. "It wasn't my fault," she yelled. "It was Ozzie's. Ask anyone."

Parker glared at his hosts' granddaughter, a deep pit of dread forming in his stomach. No doubt about it, Fiona had gotten into trouble again, and from the sound of it, she had involved Ozzie as well!

"What happened? What did you do to my horse?" he practically yelled, fending off Wolfie.

"Oh, you're here." Fiona stepped back and whipped some wet hair out of her face. "Relax. Your precious horse is just fine."

"Well?" Parker demanded. "What did you do?"

"Nothing," Fiona said, putting her hands on her hips. Seeing Parker's serious expression, she added,

"Fine. So I rode him. So he decided he felt like jumping. So I couldn't stop him. So what?"

Parker exploded. "So what? What do you mean, so what? And what do you mean, you rode him—and jumped him? Of course you couldn't stop him. He's not a beginner's horse!"

Fiona lifted her chin. "Okay, so I rode him," she flashed. "But I'm not a beginner! I've been taking lessons!"

Of all the boneheaded things! Fiona riding Ozzie? Ozzie was power-packed and unpredictable—definitely not the type of horse Fiona should ride.

"Is he hurt?" Parker asked, searching her face for the truth.

Fiona shook her head. "No, but you might ask about *me*. He turned away at the last minute and threw me right over a stone wall!"

"And if you got hurt, it served you right," Parker snapped.

Fiona pushed out her lower lip. "Well, I didn't get hurt, no thanks to your stupid horse. And by the way, you're being horrid," she huffed.

Parker frowned as Wolfie shoved his nose under his arm, wriggling with excitement. *Maybe I am*, he thought. He stroked Wolfie's wet coat. "Your dog is getting soaked, and so am I. Let's go inside, and you can fill me in on the details."

He dumped his duffel bag in the vestibule off the kitchen, took off his wet boots, and padded into the kitchen, where a teapot simmered on the Aga stove. Sighing as the comforting warmth hit him, Parker wiped the rivulets of rain from his face.

"Cup of tea?" Fiona asked. She went over to the stove, leaving wet footprints on the stone floor.

"Sure," Parker said. He slumped wearily against the oak table. "Your grandparents aren't here, are they?"

Fiona shook her head as she set a stoneware cup of steaming liquid in front of him. "Nope," she replied. "They're off at some charity event, raising money for some good cause."

Warming his hands on the hot cup of tea, Parker prodded Fiona. "Out with it. What possessed you to ride my horse, anyway? You know you weren't supposed to."

Fiona glared. "Well, *you* weren't here to ride him," she retorted.

"But I left Jack Dalton in charge of that," Parker reminded her. "You asked to turn my horses out, and I said you could. But I don't recall telling you to hop on, go for a joyride, and almost get yourself killed going over a stone wall."

Fiona sipped her tea. "Jack expected you back here sooner," she said. "He's dreadfully shorthanded as it is, and he had to go judge at a horse trial for the day. So I was just trying to help out."

Parker snorted.

"Well, I *was*," Fiona protested. "Only I wish I hadn't. That horse of yours is a frightful bounder. He won't pay attention to anything."

"He's a Nations Cup horse, for heaven's sake," Parker muttered. "Of course he's not going to pay attention to a schoolgirl."

"Well, from what I've seen, he doesn't pay that much attention to you, either," Fiona shot back. "And he even gives Jack what-for when he has a mind to."

"Just start from the beginning," Parker replied. He didn't like being reminded that he, too, had trouble getting Ozzie to pay attention.

"Well, it was early, and everyone had gone off to lunch, and I decided to try to be helpful," Fiona began. "I had turned out Ozzie like I was supposed to, but it was looking kind of cloudy, so I went to bring him in. Thing was, he had strayed to the far end of the pasture. He wouldn't let me catch him for the longest time. When I caught him finally, I was tired, and so I just kind of climbed on his back for a ride back."

Seeing Parker's look, she added, "Actually, I wasn't that tired, but I've always wanted to ride him, ever since you brought him here. I figured you'd never let me on your own, so I'd have to pinch a ride."

"Definitely not a smooth move," Parker muttered. Still, he couldn't help thinking that stealing rides on forbidden horses was exactly what he'd done when he was younger, too.

Fiona glared. "How can I tell you what happened if you keep interrupting me?"

"Go on," Parker said, lifting his cup and inhaling the steam.

"So anyway, I just sat on him for a while, then I nudged him with my heels so he'd walk about. Pretty soon we were trotting all over the place, and I didn't even have a bridle or anything," Fiona exclaimed. Parker could see the light in her eyes as she talked. "He's got the smoothest trot, you know, and he was really answering my leg.

"It wasn't till we began cantering that the problem started. All of a sudden he just took off for the fence and jumped it," Fiona went on.

"That's a surprise," Parker said sarcastically. Ozzie had escaped several times since his stay in England, and each time he had thundered across the country-side, jumping everything that came into view. Fiona herself had witnessed Ozzie's antics several times herself.

"Well, I didn't care about that," she said. "But then he decided to keep going, jumping anything that got in his way, and I couldn't stop him. But you know what? I was having so much fun, I didn't want to."

Parker was torn between being furious and wanting to nod in agreement. He felt the same way when he was jumping cross-country. He wanted the ride to go on forever.

"You know, Jack never lets me jump high enough," Fiona said, trying to plead her case with Parker. "So just when I was really getting into it, Ozzie did this big, nasty refusal at the stone wall, and I flew over it. Ozzie jumped after me and just missed squashing me with those big feet of his. Then he tore off toward the road."

"Let me guess," Parker cut in. "He ran out on the road, and he nearly got run over in traffic."

Fiona's eyes were wide. "How did you guess? There was this enormous lorry that missed him by this much," she said, putting her index finger and thumb close together.

Parker stood up, horrified at the mental picture. "You almost got my horse killed!"

"I already told you, it wasn't my fault. You know better than anyone else that Ozzie's always getting out. He very well could have jumped all those fences without me on him," Fiona pointed out. "And besides, he *didn't* get killed. He's just fine. You can go see for yourself."

"Don't ever, *ever* ride my horse again," Parker said, shaking with anger.

Fiona sipped her tea, unperturbed. "Oh, I won't," she responded. "Jack says he'll draw and quarter me right in the stable yard if I do."

"That's not nearly enough punishment," Parker shot back.

Fiona tried to look contrite. "You might be interested to know that Jack's banished me from the stable for a week."

"He ought to have banished you forever," Parker thundered. But Fiona looked so hurt that Parker instantly felt a little bad for being so harsh. After all, Ozzie wasn't hurt, and Fiona had been awfully brave to stay aboard for as long as she had. But he sure didn't want Fiona to know that was what he was thinking.

"Well, I don't see what the big deal is," Fiona said quietly. "I mean, no one was hurt, so that's all that matters."

Parker shook his head. "That's not entirely true. You know, every time Ozzie gets away with refusing and tossing his rider, he's that much more difficult to correct. I don't want to cement any more bad habits."

Fiona nodded thoughtfully. "I didn't know that," she said.

"There's a lot to learn when it comes to horses," Parker added, draining his tea. "Well, I'm going to change out of these wet clothes, and then I'm going to go down to the stable to see my horses."

"I'll come with you," Fiona said eagerly. "There's no one else here except Mrs. Smythe. I've been rattling around in this big old pile all day, and I'm lonely and bored out of my skull."

Parker grinned mischievously. "Ah, but you're banished from the stable, remember?"

Fiona stomped her foot like a five-year-old as Parker headed toward his room.

After he changed, he walked down to the stable, Wolfie bounding after him, oblivious to the rain. The dog's tongue lolled out of his mouth as he gamboled about joyously.

"Glad to see *someone's* happy," Parker said wearily as the dog charged past.

Parker knew he ought to be feeling cheerier than he was. After all, he was about to be reunited with Foxy and Ozzie at last. But thinking about what he had been through the past few days, he found himself feeling sorrier for himself than ever.

It's those two horses you ought to be sorry for, Parker reminded himself as he drew closer to the stable yard. *They're the ones who could end up God knows where.*

Jack Dalton's stable glowed eerily in the vapor lights, its massive stone buildings surrounding a stable yard that was filling with puddles. Usually the upper part of the Dutch stall doors were open, but because of the weather, they were now closed. Parker could hear the horses rustling in their straw, and occasionally he heard the thumping of a feed pan.

Pulling up the hood of his sweatshirt against the rain, Parker stepped into the warm, dry barn, hurrying down the barn aisle toward his horses' stalls.

"Hey, Foxy, hey, Ozzie," he called, his voice bouncing against the ancient walls.

Grinning as he heard Foxy's familiar whicker, Parker felt his worries lift, if only for a moment. He was back again with his beloved horses. That was all that mattered—for now.

11

"I MISSED YOU. DID YOU MISS ME?" PARKER ASKED FOXY AS he opened up her stall door.

Foxy rushed over to him, her lovely head gleaming in the light. She looked at Parker as if to say, *Where have you been all this time?*

She bumped him affectionately with her delicately tapered muzzle and proceeded to nuzzle him from the top of his head all the way to his shoulder. Giving him a slobbery kiss on his sweatshirt, she then thrust her nose into his pocket, searching for her favorite treats.

"Polo mints, coming right up," Parker said with a laugh as he took out a roll. "Only one for now. After all the work Jack has done setting up a feeding plan for you, we don't want you scarfing down too many treats."

Parker smiled and adjusted the straps on Foxy's thick blanket while she crunched contentedly. He fluffed her thick bedding for a few moments and then just stood quietly in her stall, basking in her presence. The last few days of worry and guilt seemed to float away as he breathed in her warm, horsy scent. Leaning against her, he wrapped his arms around her sleek neck.

"Foxy, you are the best," he murmured, feeling her silky coat against his cheek.

Closing his eyes, he pictured himself tacking her up in the morning. He could hardly wait to climb into the saddle and take her on a long ride. A fitness gallop, perhaps. Or he could jump her over the cross-country course. Maybe he'd ride her on a steeplechase course. He could feel the adrenaline surging through his body just thinking about it.

"What about it, girl?" he asked Foxy. "Are you raring to jump as much as I am?"

A few minutes later Parker walked over to Ozzie's stall.

"Hey, you," he said softly. "I've been hearing troubling reports about you, big guy."

The gelding stood there regarding him goofily, some wisps of hay dangling from his mouth. His new

133

blanket was already patched in several places, and Parker sighed. "You big lug," he said fondly as he unlatched Ozzie's stall door and stepped inside. He looked more closely at the blanket and shook his head. "Tearing up your blanket as usual, I see. You'd better make it last a while longer. I'm not made of money, you know. I'm already almost bankrupt paying for all the things you destroy around here."

Ozzie let out a huge breath and proceeded to shift his weight, stepping soundly on Parker's foot with his giant front hoof.

"Ouch," Parker cried, pulling his foot out. "That's no way to greet the person who pays your feed bill."

Ozzie hung his head, his large ears flopping, while Parker wiggled his sore toes. Reaching up, Parker traced the jagged scar just above the gelding's nostril. "Oh, I know you didn't mean it," Parker added. "But you *do* have some explaining to do about those other rumors I've been hearing."

Ozzie regarded Parker with big brown eyes. "Trying to look innocent?" Parker laughed. "C'mon, I know all about how you carted Fiona across the countryside, acting like a puissance jumper. That definitely wasn't cool."

Ozzie snorted and then turned away, his big rump practically swinging into Parker's face. He switched his black tail impudently for good measure.

"I know, I know," Parker said, laughing. "Fiona was acting like a horse's behind, climbing on your back without so much as a by-your-leave. I'm just glad she didn't get both of you killed."

Parker sighed as he looked at Ozzie. This big gelding and Foxy were such vastly different horses, in terms of both looks and personality. Foxy was exciting and bold but refined and elegant at the same time. Ozzie was a total doof, but when he was on, there was no stopping him.

Well, I'm glad I'm back and can get on with taking care of both of them properly, Parker thought. *I've just got to put the past behind me and think only about what's ahead.*

At the sound of footsteps Ozzie threw his head up. Parker looked out of the stall and saw Jack Dalton heading down the barn aisle.

Oh, great. What is he doing here so late? Parker had figured he wouldn't have to deal with his instructor until the morning. He was too tired to have to face the lecture he was sure to receive.

"Well, now, isn't this a surprise. I see that our world traveler is back," Dalton said wryly. A tall man with red hair, Dalton was dressed in his usual pressed breeches topped with a Barbour jacket. Where he normally wore highly polished knee boots, he was now wearing muddy Wellingtons. "And not a moment too soon, I might add."

Parker patted Ozzie's shoulder reluctantly and stepped out of the stall. The last thing he wanted to do was face the stern instructor and hear how far behind he was in his training. As if he didn't know that already!

"I'm back, and you're right, not a moment too soon," Parker replied evenly.

Just then Ozzie thrust his big head through the opened door, snorting violently and pressing Parker up to the door frame.

"I suppose you've already heard about this old boy's latest escapade," Dalton said, scratching his jaw. "I can't decide if I should call his partner in crime Fearless Fiona or Foolish Fiona."

"I vote for Foolish Fiona," Parker replied. "I'm going to make sure she stays far away from my horses in the future. I've got enough problems without her adding to them."

Dalton rubbed his jaw. "Very true," he said. "Of course, the way I see it, your biggest problem is that you think you want to ride in the Olympics someday, but you're not willing to stay focused."

"I am too!" Parker protested.

"All evidence to the contrary," Dalton countered. "Along comes the Triple Crown, and you decide to abandon ship and flit across the ocean to be a spectator."

"I needed to go," Parker shot back.

Jack continued. "Then a maggot enters your head, and you decide to pop over to Kentucky instead of returning on schedule—and, worse, extend your stay. Never mind two high-strung horses that need high-level work and intensive conditioning. You're off on yet another jaunt! Come to think of it, you're rather like Ozzie in that regard."

Parker felt the sting of his words sharply. "That's not fair," he protested feebly. It wasn't like that at all. But he couldn't help realizing that that was how it must look to Dalton. "I mean, I'm here now, and I'm ready to make up for the lost time," he added in a tight voice.

"Lost time is never regained," Dalton countered sourly. "It's a little over a month and a half till Burghley, and there's loads of work to be done. Foxglove is coming along nicely, of course, but she'll have to be at the top of her game if you two are going to take on the competition."

Squinting, he peered at Parker closely. "Maybe you need a reminder: The stakes are high here. The best riders from all over the world will be at Burghley. They've all got drive, determination, and talented horses to spare. Foxglove is no doubt a contender, but I don't need to tell you that your second horse is a loose cannon."

137

"But I'm bringing only Foxy to Burghley," Parker protested. "That was always the plan."

Dalton scratched his jaw. "I'm thinking beyond Burghley, of course. I don't need to remind you that if you're really Olympic material, you've got to think ahead. You've always got to have prospects in the wings, ready just in case. There are no guarantees, no sure things. Pinning all your hopes on one horse— even one as fabulous as Foxglove—is risky business."

Pictures of the two Welton horses flashed unbidden in Parker's mind. What would Jack say if he knew that Parker had turned down two of the best prospects on the eventing scene?

"I'll have Ozzie ready when the time comes, as well as Foxy," Parker muttered. "Ozzie's got what it takes. It just takes some horses a little longer to get there."

"Fact is, it's not even about the horses," Jack said quietly. "I'm more concerned about whether you've got what it takes." He folded his arms across his chest and looked straight at Parker. "I had a little chat with Captain Donnelly last night, and I told him that I'm not sure you're what they call around here a gamer, someone who *tries*."

"I *do* try!" Parker replied, his voice rising.

Dalton rubbed his jaw. "When all's said and done, I think you lack the passion you need to succeed at this sport. And that's something I don't have any control over. If you're lacking it in the first place, there's nothing I can do."

A deep anger surged through Parker. Was he being dumped? Was he going to have to shelve his Olympic dream and fly home, tail tucked between his legs? Oh, how his father would chortle at that. Parker's reputation would be ruined, and he'd have to sign on to work at Townsend Acres just to keep from starving.

And since Fanfaer and Black Hawke had been sold, it wouldn't cost his dad the big bucks after all to tie him down. *As it turns out, there* is *such a thing as a free lunch*, Parker could imagine Brad saying.

"Fine," Parker fired back at Dalton. "Dump me if you want. But I'll have you know that I'm still going to ride at Burghley, and I'll be riding to win. So what if I have to do it on my own? No one is going to stop me." *Even you, Dad!* he added silently.

Dalton's face twitched, as though he was trying not to smile. "You'd go take on Burghley just like that, huh?"

Parker nodded. "Yeah, I would. I've worked for years making Foxy into the best eventer around. I've battled through almost every obstacle imaginable. I've defied my family, I've scraped by with no money, I've given up almost everything else in my life. If you believe I'd give up just because *you* didn't think I could do it, well, you've got another think coming!"

Dalton grinned. "Huh. Maybe you *are* a gamer after all."

But Parker hadn't finished. "Look, it might seem to you that I'm playing around and jetting off to watch a few horse races and hang out with my buddies in Kentucky, but it's not like that at all."

Jack arched an eyebrow at him. "What's it like, then?"

"I had some important unfinished business to attend to, first in New York, then in Kentucky," Parker began.

"Go on," Dalton urged.

The two of them sat on some overturned buckets, and Parker told him the whole story, starting with Christina and finishing with his last good-bye to two never-to-be-forgotten horses. "Now they're probably standing in some low-rent auction barn wondering why they're homeless yet again!" Parker said sadly. And though he felt guilty about it, Parker made no effort to whitewash his dad's role in the whole chain of events.

"If my dad hadn't been injured, I might not have been so weak," Parker ended lamely. His voice was hoarse, and he felt more tired than he ever had in his life.

Dalton stood up. "That's some story," he said. "I'm going to go home now and think about what you've said. It's late, and my wife will be wondering what's keeping me." And then Dalton smiled with uncharacteristic gentleness in his eyes. "I'll expect you to be here at daybreak, ready to work."

Parker felt relief flooding him. He wasn't being dumped after all! He still had one more chance.

Walking back to Kempton Hall, Parker felt a flicker of hope inside him. And it wasn't even dampened by the rain pelting his face.

12

THE NEXT MORNING PARKER WAS UP BEFORE DAWN.
Though he was jet-lagged and had once again found
himself tossing and turning instead of sleeping, he
dragged himself out of bed and jumped into his riding
clothes. He raced down the curving staircase and
stopped at the landing. Looking out the leaded-glass
panes, Parker saw that the rain had given way to the
promise of a glorious morning. And he knew it was
going to be a beautiful day.

"Morning, Mrs. Smythe," he called to the kindly
housekeeper as she entered the kitchen.

"Good to see you, lad," she said with a smile.
"How are things in the States?"

"Just great," Parker lied.

He fixed himself a protein shake and headed out to the stable, sucking down his breakfast. He was determined to stay upbeat and focused. He was going to show Jack Dalton just what a gamer he was.

Parker stepped into the barn and spotted Charlie Simms, Dalton's assistant, checking the scheduling board.

"If it isn't the incredible disappearing Yank," Simms grunted. Although Parker and Simms had been getting along better since the Merebrook horse trial, they still weren't particularly chummy. That was fine by Parker. He got along with practically everyone else, and anyway, he was there to work, not buddy up to everyone.

"I've reappeared," Parker replied. "Where does Dalton want me to get started?"

"You're to work in the dressage arena today," Simms called out, still facing the board. His thin mouth turned up in just the barest hint of a smirk.

Jerk, Parker thought. *Simms knows I'd rather jump than work on dressage. But he also knows I'm in no position to say anything to Dalton.*

"Thanks," Parker said, forcing a smile. He wouldn't give Simms the satisfaction of seeing his annoyance.

Stepping into Foxy's stall, Parker unblanketed her and led her to the crossties. Then he hooked her to the ties and picked up his grooming box.

Foxy's summer coat was beautiful to behold—and it definitely was easier to groom than her longer winter one. Parker didn't need to use a currycomb at all. Instead he brought out a firm brush and ran it lightly over her gleaming hide. Afterward he smoothed it with a soft body brush. Finally he went over her one more time with a soft cloth.

"You look fit and fabulous as ever, girl." Parker stood back to admire his handiwork.

Bending over to pick up Foxy's front left foot, he frowned. "But from the looks of it, you're about due for new shoes." *Oh, yay. Just what I need—a shoeing bill,* Parker thought, picking out each of her well-shaped hooves.

When he was finished, Parker cleaned out Foxy's ears and nostrils with a soft, clean cotton cloth. He was just tacking her up when Thomas appeared. The thin groom broke into a grin when he saw Parker. "Glad you're back," he said, tipping his trilby hat. His eyes twinkled mischievously. "Now maybe that great big horse of yours will behave himself for a bit."

"I wouldn't count on it," Parker said with a sigh, placing Foxy's dressage saddle on her back and beginning to buckle the girth loosely.

Thomas chuckled and ducked into a nearby stall, humming "Danny Boy" under his breath. Seconds later he emerged leading a prancing chestnut.

Parker slipped Foxy's bridle over her head. Smiling as Foxy bobbed her head, Parker fastened the noseband. "I don't like dressage any more than you do," he confided to his mare. "But we'd better stay on Dalton's good side from here on out, so no complaints, okay?"

Although Parker would have preferred to work on the cross-country course, he knew he definitely needed more work on dressage. It was usually his weakest score in competition.

After Parker warmed up Foxy, taking her through each gait and executing several transitions, Dalton walked into the center of the arena.

"Are you ready to work?" the instructor barked out.

I'm in for it now, Parker thought. *It's payback time for my being away.* But aloud he said only, "Yes, sir."

Hours later an exhausted Parker emerged from the barn after intense dressage sessions on both Foxy and Ozzie. Not having ridden for the last several days, other than a brief school on Scooter, had taken a toll on Parker's stamina. He was sure that Dalton knew how tired he must be, but still the instructor was relentless.

"Do it again," Dalton had shouted whenever Parker administered a sloppy cue.

Parker rounded the corner by the clock tower and ran into Phillipa pushing a portable saddle rack.

"Hey, Parker, you're back!" the groom said happily, brushing back her dark, sweaty bangs.

Parker nodded. "Yeah. I got in last night."

"Great. We're all going to the movies tonight. Want to come?"

"Sure, thanks," Parker said. *If I'm still alive by then*, he added silently. He was already wiped out, but he didn't want everyone at the stable to think he was a stick-in-the-mud.

"We're meeting here at eight," Phillipa replied. "See you then!"

A few minutes later Parker sat on a mounting block outside the main arena, sipping a bottle of cold water and resting his screaming muscles.

At the sound of approaching hoofbeats, he looked up. It was Fiona, leading Fable, a gentle chestnut who was usually given to beginners. Fable was tacked up, and Fiona was wearing breeches, boots, and a jersey. She held her velvet hunt cap and gloves in her hand.

"I thought you were banished," Parker called out.

Fiona threw him a triumphant smile. "I talked my way out of it," she said. "I promised Dalton that I'd never, ever try anything like riding Ozzie again. Oh, and I had to promise to clean all the school's tack for the next month. Ugh."

"I can't believe Dalton fell for your promises," Parker replied, rolling his eyes. "I guess being born to nobility sure has its perks."

Fiona glared at him. "It wasn't that," she said. "It was that Jack could see how much I missed The Lion."

Parker snorted. He knew that Jack, like the Chillinghams, had a soft spot for the girl, believing that she really meant well. As for himself, he wasn't sure what to believe when it came to Fiona.

"Push off," she said, stuffing her blond hair under her hunt cap. "I need the mounting block."

Parker stood up and walked a few steps away, wincing as pain shot up his calves and through his thighs. As soon as Fiona mounted, Parker saw Fable's ears flatten.

"He's as crabby as you are," Fiona grumbled, adjusting her feet in the stirrups.

"Something's wrong," Parker began as Fable backed up quickly, then bucked three times in succession.

"You're a frightful pain," Fiona said, pulling up on the reins sharply.

"Stop jerking on the reins," Parker called out. "You're hurting his mouth. Sit back!"

Just then Fable sank slowly to his knees.

"Kick your feet out of the stirrups," Parker commanded Fiona. "He's going to go on his side. Get out of the way—*now*."

Fiona freed her feet from her stirrups and rolled away just as the horse hit the ground.

Fable thrashed on the ground for a moment, then stood up, shaking himself mightily.

"He was trying to shed me!" Fiona said accusingly, scrambling to her feet and dusting herself off.

Parker raced over to Fable. Pulling up the near saddle flap, he saw the problem immediately. "You pulled his girth too tight!" he exclaimed. "No wonder the poor horse went down. He could hardly breathe."

"Oh," Fiona replied, hanging her head. "I didn't know I'd done it up too tight. Last time I had it too loose, and the saddle slipped and I fell off."

Parker shook his head and ran his hands over Fable's legs to make sure nothing else had happened. He pulled the reins over the chestnut's head and walked the horse for a few minutes to allow him to catch his breath. After he'd adjusted the girth, he told Fiona to come over and mount up again.

"First," he said sternly, "check your girth. You want to be able to fit a couple of fingers between Fable's side and the girth. If it's too tight, it's quite painful."

Fiona nodded and climbed aboard. "It was an accident, but I feel terrible," she said, looking shamefaced as she patted Fable's neck apologetically. "I didn't know I was hurting him."

Parker's eyes followed Fiona as she rode Fable toward the ring, and he felt a wave of sadness wash over him. Once again he was reminded how easy it was to hurt a horse even if you didn't intend to.

Just like I might have done to Black Hawke and Fanfaer.

By walking out on his dad, had he sentenced them to an uncaring home where they might be mistreated?

That evening Parker sat in the oak-paneled library with Hilyard Chillingham and Fiona, watching a video of The Lion competing in Badminton. His host was clearly very proud of his talented horse and stopped the video every few seconds to point out some detail to Parker. Though The Lion's win was incredibly exciting, Parker was having a hard time staying awake.

"Now, look at this," Chillingham exclaimed, pointing at the way the black horse used his hindquarters to push off in a mighty effort at a treacherous water jump. "It was an accurate ride that gave The Lion the firepower he needed right then."

Parker leaned forward and tried to focus on what Chillingham was saying. But in spite of a monumental effort, it was getting harder and harder to keep his eyes open. Maybe he'd just rest his eyes for a second. . . .

The bright sunlight streamed in through the window directly into Parker's eyes. He blinked. *Hey! Where is everyone, and why is it so sunny?*

It was morning. Parker was so exhausted, he'd fallen asleep right there in his chair. But even though he'd slept curled up on the chair, he felt strangely rested and ready to go.

Half an hour later, after washing his face and grabbing breakfast, Parker walked into the tack room. "Turn in early, don't we?" Phillipa teased.

"I'm so sorry," Parker said, picking up his equipment. "I said I'd go to the movies with you all, and then I never showed up!"

She looked around to make sure no one was listening. "Dalton's being pretty beastly to you, isn't he," she whispered conspiratorially.

Parker shook his head. "Yeah. Well, no," he said, though every muscle in his body was aching. "He's just trying to make sure I want Burghley bad enough."

Phillipa rolled her eyes. "He can be a taskmaster, all right." She whipped a couple of bridles off their racks and stepped out of the tack room.

You can say that again, Parker thought. *I wonder*

what's in store for me today. But suddenly he felt a surge of excitement and broke out in a grin. Whatever Dalton dished out, he could handle it.

"Bring it on," Parker whispered out loud. He picked up his grooming box and went to check out the scheduling board.

The next few days were grueling, as Dalton continually stepped up his demands. He drilled Parker mercilessly in the dressage arena, making him stop and correct every slight misstep. When it came to cross-country, he set up technically difficult courses that tested Parker to the limit. During stadium-jumping sessions he had Parker jump the fences again and again, all the while bellowing, "Timing! Timing!"

More than once Parker found himself on the ground, but he picked himself up quickly and gritted his teeth as he climbed back on, determined to get it right this time.

"Not quite at your best, are you?" Dalton would goad him.

Parker knew Dalton was only trying to inspire him to work harder, but it still annoyed him. Parker had assumed that once Dalton heard his story, he'd have some sympathy. But day by day, it was becoming clear that he didn't.

"I think he's forgotten he's supposed to be helping me ride better. Instead he's just trying to kill me," Parker confessed to Fiona after a particularly grueling day. He didn't usually confide in her, but he was so worn out that he just needed someone to talk to.

Fiona nodded. "He's sure giving you a workout."

Parker rubbed his shoulder where it ached after a spill he'd taken earlier in the day. "Even on my horses' day off, he puts me on the greenest horses he can find and has me jump that crazy course he's set up. I've never seen anything like it," he added. "Even the course at Rolex seemed easier than those monsters Jack has me going over, especially on those squirrelly firecrackers he calls horses."

"I'd rather do what you're doing than have to ride fat old Fable around," Fiona said enviously. "It's like riding a tortoise. You're riding for real. I'd *love* to do that."

Parker had to admit she had a point there—riding a spirited horse *was* an amazing feeling. "I understand what you mean, Fiona. Held back. That's how I used to feel," he said. "But I was watching you for a few minutes this morning, and you're getting better. So maybe soon you'll be able to move on to more difficult horses."

Fiona's eyes shone at the unexpected praise. "You really think so?" she said eagerly.

"I know so," Parker replied. "And believe it or not, a horse like Fable isn't easy to ride. He requires a lot of leg, and you seem to know right away when he's sucking back and trying to evade your aids. You really make him a better horse than he is."

Fiona seemed to drink in his words. "I like it a lot better when he's energized from behind. It's a lot less work that way."

Parker nodded. "You might surprise all of us yet and be able to ride a more advanced horse like The Lion one of these days."

"I hope so," Fiona breathed reverently. Then she tilted her head. "I overheard Dalton tell Simms the other day that you were coming along nicely."

"He said that, huh?" Parker couldn't help grinning. "To my face, he tells me that I ought to take up knitting."

"He does not!" Fiona laughed with delight.

"Well, maybe not in those words," Parker joked.

"He just doesn't want you to get all puffed up about yourself the way you were when you first came here," Fiona said.

"I wasn't all puffed up," protested Parker, though even as he spoke the words he knew that what Fiona had said was for all intents and purposes true.

"Ha!" Fiona countered. "I gave you my own private nickname: Count Conceit!"

Parker rammed her playfully with his good shoulder on his way out of the room. "Who's talking, Princess Chillingham?" he cracked over his shoulder.

As he headed down the vestibule toward the kitchen, he thought, *Wow, it seems as though we're actually getting along.* Parker smiled. Maybe Connie was right. It *could* be kind of nice to have a little sister around, even if she was annoying at times.

The next few days were filled with more of Jack Dalton's special brand of torture. Each night Parker dropped into bed exhausted. Embarrassed that he couldn't even summon up the energy to talk with his hosts at dinner, he began taking his meals in his room. He watched videos of all the top events—Badminton, Rolex, Burghley, and more—taking lengthy notes while he ate.

More than once he woke up to find that he'd fallen asleep in front of the TV. Yet, busy as he was, Black Hawke and Fanfaer popped into Parker's head at the oddest moments. He would be bathing Ozzie in the wash racks when Ozzie's wet coat would suddenly remind him of the way Fanfaer's coat had glistened in the sun that day. He'd hear Foxy's whicker and remember how Black Hawke had whickered the last time he'd seen him.

Whenever Parker thought about them and all the terrible things that could be happening to them, his mood would plunge. *I wonder where they are now,* he'd think. *I sure hope they've found good homes.*

Every day Parker meant to call home and find out how his father was doing. But every time he reached for the phone he stopped himself—surely if his dad were worse, his mother would call. Then a sour feeling would fill his stomach, and guilt would envelop him for hours. The sole thing that could take his mind off it was going to the stable and working himself extra hard.

The only bright spots in his days were when Foxy and Ozzie would go particularly well during a schooling session, or the rare occasions when he would talk to Christina on the phone.

But as the next two weeks passed in a blur of hard work, he became more and more aware that Burghley was getting closer—and time was running out.

13

"I DON'T GET IT," GRUMBLED FIONA, GIVING PARKER A pouty look. "You used to be jolly and a joke a minute. But ever since you've gotten back, you're a real cross-patch." It was late Saturday afternoon, and Fiona and Parker were heading down to the stable after brunch up at the house. The Chillinghams had insisted they both attend. "We've invited all our horse-loving friends, some of them fine eventers themselves, and they're dying to meet you," Nancy Chillingham had told Parker the night before.

Normally Parker loved a good party, especially one filled with eventing enthusiasts. He was a great story-teller and usually ended up surrounded by a crowd of people absorbed in his entertaining tales of horses and horse people.

That day, however, he had wanted only to retreat from conversation with well-meaning strangers, dodge the endless questions about his chances at Burghley, and escape from the noisy festivities. He couldn't wait to return to the stable.

"Guess I wasn't much fun at your grandparents' get-together," Parker said to Fiona as he rubbed his pounding temples. The music and the laughter had given him a rare headache, and he wished Fiona wouldn't talk so much.

"You can say that again," Fiona snorted.

"Fine, so I'm not a laugh a minute," Parker muttered while increasing his pace. "Can you blame me? I'm being run into the ground by your pal Jack Dalton."

"Slow down," complained Fiona, trotting to catch up with him. "I don't see why you're in such a hurry to come back to the stable, anyway. You've been spending every waking minute with your horses as it is."

"Oh, Fiona," Parker replied, exasperated. "How can I ever explain to you what winning Burghley means to me?"

Fiona put her hands on her hips. "I think you're obsessed," she said. "I've never seen anything like it."

Fiona was right. It *was* an obsession. Parker looked

around him at the hedgerows, the stone walls, and the green fields beyond. Whereas other people would see a picturesque English countryside, all he saw were logs, gates, and fences—obstacles to be jumped. And, of course, every time he thought of jumping, he thought of Burghley and the members of the Olympic selection committee, who would be scouting for talented horses and riders.

Talented riders with their own string of talented horses, he corrected himself.

As Parker walked on, he fell into a deep gloom. Working so hard on Foxy and Ozzie in preparation for the big event had also been a kind of escape. As long as he was worrying about smooth transitions and the rhythmic pounding of endless fitness gallops, he didn't have to think about other things. He could take all his concerns about his father's accident and all the pressure of the competition and push them to the back of his head. But now that he was making his way back to the barn, the full force of what he was up against was hitting him in the face. Even if he won Burghley and was finally selected for the Olympic team, he knew that it could all blow up in his face if Ozzie didn't pan out or Foxy so much as pulled a ligament and ended up lame at the wrong time. All of his hard work and his dramatic grandstanding to his dad would have been for nothing.

"I'm talking to you." Fiona's voice cut into Parker's thoughts.

"Sorry," he said politely. "I was just thinking about something."

"And I was just talking about something, and you're being horribly rude," Fiona grumbled.

"Uh-huh." Parker sighed and tried to listen.

"It's The Lion," Fiona said, chattering quickly now that she had Parker's attention.

"The Lion again? What about him?" Parker rolled his eyes. Couldn't Fiona ever bring up another subject? Fiona was always talking about him as if he were her horse.

"Well, I was just thinking that I really want to buy him from my grandfather," she said.

Parker shot her a look.

"Your grandfather would never sell The Lion. Never in a million years."

Fiona blew out a noisy breath. "I know it," she said wistfully. "Don't you think it's beastly of him to hog that horse all for himself?"

"Why shouldn't he keep his horse? He's crazy about him. Talks of nothing else other than The Lion winning Badminton and all. You can't seriously believe he'd sell him to you," Parker said.

"Well, aren't grandfathers supposed to do nice things like that?"

"You're a horrid, spoiled girl," Parker said, looking at her in amusement.

"Well, so are you!" Fiona fired back.

Just then Parker noticed that Fiona's eyes were sparkling and that she was practically dancing on the toes of her paddock boots.

As they neared the well-manicured stable Fiona suddenly stopped and grabbed his arm. "Let's go over to the paddocks first," she said.

"Why?" Parker asked, annoyed. He just wanted to be left alone and go groom Foxy for a while. "I don't have time to mess around. I need to go thin Foxy's mane."

"Just for a minute," Fiona insisted. "I want to show you something."

"Fine," Parker grunted. Reluctantly he turned toward the paddocks, Fiona skipping ahead.

Just like Wolfie, Parker thought. Sometimes he found it hard to believe that his hosts' granddaughter was fifteen. At that moment she was acting like a little girl on Christmas morning. *What's she up to now?*

"You haven't done anything to either of my horses, have you?" Parker was suddenly suspicious. It was just like Fiona to try something like thinning Foxy's mane herself, thinking she was being a help.

Fiona turned to look over her shoulder at him.

"Look," she said, pointing toward the paddock. Off

in the distance Parker could see Jack Dalton and Simms standing next to a black horse. Dalton held the lead rope, and Simms was bending over the horse, running his hands down his wide, flat cannons.

"Well?" Fiona demanded, her eyes shining.

"Why are you showing me The Lion?"

Fiona wrinkled her snub nose and shook her head. "It's not The Lion. Honestly, Parker, you can be as thick as a plank. Look again," she said.

When Parker did so, his jaw dropped. *It was Black Hawke!*

"Huh?" Parker gasped.

"Simms's eyes popped out of their sockets when they unloaded him in the yard," Fiona was saying, but Parker hardly heard her. "He said, 'That Parker Townsend has all the luck.'"

Just then Dalton noticed Parker, and he and Simms led Hawke over. "I take it you know this horse?" he said in a dry voice.

"Sure do. But I don't get it," sputtered Parker. "What's he doing here in England?"

Fiona danced around him gleefully. "I told you he'd be surprised!"

"Maybe this gentleman can enlighten you," Dalton said, jerking his chin toward a thin, tweed-clad figure who was approaching them from across the field. The figure disappeared as the field dipped, then reap-

161

peared. Suddenly Parker recognized who it was—his grandfather! Coming closer, Clay held out his gnarled, work-worn hand and motioned Parker over to him.

"I thought you were in Ireland!" Parker exclaimed, his head spinning as he leaped over the fence and rushed up to embrace his grandfather in a hug. His gaze darted over to the black horse and back to Clay again.

Clay nodded, laughter crinkling up the corners of his eyes. "I was, till some business brought me down here. And before I knew it, it was time to deliver a horse to you," he replied. "Seems that son of mine was meddling in your life again, and in the process he meddled with a couple of very fine horses as well."

Still stunned, Parker walked over to Black Hawke and took the lead rope from Simms. "But how did you know?" he asked, reaching over to stroke the horse's smooth, arched neck.

Clay shrugged. "It took a little digging around," he admitted. "Something didn't sit quite right with me after you and I talked, so I called to talk to my son, and got my daughter-in-law instead. She was pretty cagey with me, but I got her to admit that Brad's accident was not as serious as they were playing it up to be. A mild concussion, that was it."

"Well, it *could* have been much more serious,"

Parker said doubtfully. "I keep thinking about when Tabasco Cat ran over Wayne Lukas's son."

Clay nodded. "Perhaps, but the point is that Brad *wasn't* hurt—yet he pretended shamefully and used his injury to try to manipulate you. And knowing my son and how determined he is, I figured that if he was trying to trick you with an exaggerated accident, he probably had backup plans as well. Then when I heard he was selling these horses, I wondered what he was doing with this pair when they're clearly *not* race-horses. So I put two and two together and figured he must have been trying to bribe you to stay. And I knew how much they must mean to you, so—"

"But, Grandfather," Parker interrupted, "you didn't have to!"

Clay held up his hand and motioned for Parker to let him continue. "By the time my agent got to the sorry auction house he'd sent them to, someone named Breen had snapped up Fanfaer, but I managed to win the bidding on this dazzling piece of horseflesh here," Clay said. "That Breen guy wasn't happy that my wallet was fatter than his, but he ought to be content with Fanfaer."

Parker smiled in spite of himself. His pal David Breen must have gotten the message Parker left on the window!

"I pulled a few strings to speed Hawke through quarantine and arranged to have him shipped here so that you could turn him into a world-class eventer—if you're so inclined," the old horseman said.

Parker was speechless.

"You *are* still inclined, aren't you?" Clay asked with a smile.

"Of course I am!" Parker said, his eyes shining brightly. "But, Grandfather, you didn't have to go to all this trouble to buy Black Hawke for me."

Clay took off his hat and ran his hand through his silvery hair. "No, I didn't *have* to," he agreed. "I'd lay money on the fact that Foxy will be your top Olympic horse, but it never hurts to have a prospect or two in the wings if you're going to be in the eventing business for the long haul."

"No, I mean you didn't have to shell out to buy me another horse," Parker said with a sudden rush of emotion. "You've—you've already been so good to me, giving me Foxy, sending me a ticket so I could see the Triple Crown, and all the other stuff you've done over the years. I can't keep accepting gifts from you. I should be able to do things on my own."

Clay patted his back affectionately. "I like your independent spirit, boy," he said. "But you've got lofty goals here, and it doesn't hurt to get a little help along the way when it comes to going after something so big. And what is family for, anyway, if not to help out at times?"

Parker looked searchingly into his grandfather's face. "I'll never be able to thank you enough," he said quietly.

"Just work hard and make me proud, like you always have," Clay replied. Then, clearing his throat, he turned to regard Black Hawke, who had dropped his head and was now grazing contentedly. "Well, that certainly is quite a horse you've got there, my boy."

Parker's gaze rested on the statuesque black horse. *I can't believe this horse is mine,* he thought.

And then at the sound of a shrill, trumpeting whinny, he looked up toward the next paddock, where Foxy and Ozzie were standing at the fence, trying to get his attention.

"Excuse me for a moment," he said, and hurried over to his two other magnificent horses.

"You don't have a thing to worry about," Parker murmured to Foxy. "You'll always be number one with me, and Ozzie, you're an awfully close second, even if you're a great big pain. But isn't it nice to know there's someone else on our side?"

When he stopped to think about it, Parker realized he had *lots* of someones on his side. Even though his relationship with his father was less than solid, he had a great girlfriend, a loving grandfather, and a host of mentors and friends who would be cheering him on at Burghley—and beyond. It was an unbeatable combination.

Parker gazed at his three wonderful horses and smiled broadly. "Look out, Olympics, here I come!"

Lucy Thompson on Welton Romance, European Championships, Pratoni, Italy, 1995

The Welton line is one of the most famous lines in the world of British eventing. Many horses from this line have competed and won titles at the international level.

Pictured above is a well-known mare from the Welton line, Welton Romance. Bred by the famous Sam Barr and sired by Welton Louis, Welton Romance was born in 1985. She is owned by Lucy Thompson, a former three-day event competitor. Welton Romance was the Open European champion from 1995 through 1997. She is the only mare to have won a major eventing championship. She was the top-graded mare in 1999.

Karle Dickerson grew up riding, reading, writing, and dreaming about horses. This is the seventh horse book she has written. She has shown in hunters and dressage, worked at a Thoroughbred breeding farm, and has been on cattle drives in Wyoming. She and her family used to own a horse ranch, and have always had numerous horses and ponies. The latest include two Thoroughbreds off the track named Cezanne and Earl Gray, and a gray Welsh pony named Magpie.